The Prince of Rags and Patches

D1579410

Terry Deary was born in Sunderland and now lives in County Durham, where the Marsdens of *Tudor Terror* lived. Once an actor, he has also been a teacher of English and drama and has led hundreds of workshops for children in schools. He is the author of the phenomenally bestselling *Horrible Histories* and of many other successful books for children, both fiction and non-fiction.

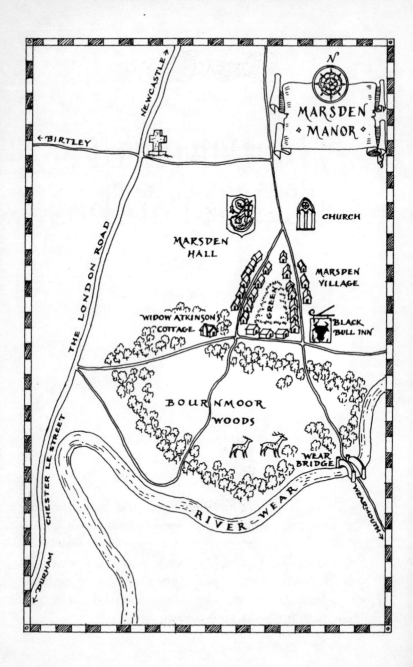

The Prince of Rags and Patches

Terry Deary

Illustrated by Hemesh Alles

Orion Children's Books
and
Dolphin Paperbacks

First published in Great Britain in 1997
as an Orion hardback
and a Dolphin paperback

by Orion Children's Books
a division of the Orion Publishing Group Ltd
Orion House
5 Upper St Martin's Lane
London WC2H 9EA

Third impression 1998

A catalogue record for this book is available
from the British Library

Typeset at The Spartan Press Ltd,
Lymington, Hants

Printed in Great Britain by Clays Ltd, St Ives plc

ISBN 1 85881 514 2 (hb)
ISBN 1 85881 515 0 (pb)

Contents

All chapter titles are quotations from plays
by William Shakespeare

The Marsden Family

WILLIAM MARSDEN *The narrator*
The youngest member of the family. Training to be a knight as his ancestors were before him, although the great days of knighthood are long gone. His father insists on it and Great-Uncle George hopes for it. But he'd rather be an actor like the travelling players he has seen in the city. He can dream.

Grandmother **LADY ELEANOR MARSDEN**
She was a lady-in-waiting to Queen Anne Boleyn. After seeing the fate of her mistress she came to hate all men, she married one, maybe out of revenge. Behind her sharp tongue there is a sharper brain. She is wiser than she looks.

Grandfather **SIR CLIFFORD MARSDEN**
He was a soldier in Henry VIII's army where (Grandmother says) the batterings softened his brain. Sir Clifford is the head of the family although he does not manage the estate these days he simply looks after the money it makes. He is well known for throwing his gold around like an armless man.

Great-Uncle **SIR GEORGE SULGRAVE**
A knight who lost his lands and now lives
with his stepsister, Grandmother Marsden.
He lives in the past and enjoys fifty-year-old
stories as much as he enjoys fifty-year-old
wine. He never lets the truth stand in the way of
a good story.

SIR JAMES MARSDEN *William's father*
He runs the Marsden estate and is magistrate for the district. He believes that, without him, the forces of evil would take over
the whole of the land. This makes him a
harsh and humourless judge. As a result he is
as popular as the plague.

LADY MARSDEN *William's mother*
She was a lady-in-waiting to Mary Queen of
Scots. Then she married Sir James. No one
quite knows why. She is beautiful, intelligent,
caring and witty. Quite the opposite of her
husband and everyone else in the house.

MARGARET "MEG" LUMLEY
Not a member of the family, but needs to be included
for she seems to be involved in all the family
tales. A poor peasant and serving girl, but
bright, fearless and honest (she says). Also
beautiful under her weather-stained skin
and the most loyal friend any family could
wish for (she says).

CHAPTER ONE

"So full of dismal terror was the time"

I remember the time when the great Queen Elizabeth was dying. The time when I lived at Marsden Hall in the north-east of England with my family. I remember it was a time of tales.

There was an ancient custom in the Marsden family. Every evening after supper they would tell stories. In summer they'd walk in the walled garden and sit in the shade of the oak tree that was older than the house itself.

"The first house was burned down by William the Conqueror," my Great-Uncle George used to say. He was the oldest of the family. Even older than Grandfather Marsden.

"How do you know?" Grandmother Marsden always snapped back at him. "I suppose you were with William the Conqueror when he did it? Were you? You old liar!" She hated him the way all good sisters hate their older stepbrothers.

She pulled back her lips as if she wanted to bite him ... but she only bared pale pink gums. Great-Uncle George mocked her by showing his fine, strong yellow teeth in an evil grin. "Go suck on a bone, you miserable trout," he smiled. He loved her too.

Father stepped between the two. "I am guardian of the

peace in this region," he said. "I must be seen as a man of peace." My father was as cold as a North Sea herring.

"When I was a magistrate I kept the peace with my sword," said Grandfather Marsden. "Nothing like a smack on the back of the head to knock the villainy out of some cutpurse or prigger!"

"One of them must have smacked you back," Granny Marsden sneered. "That's why you're such an old buffle-head!"

Mother would take her sewing and smile quietly over it. She knew that when the arguing had died down someone would say, "I remember …"

And those magic words were like the shadow of a hawk on a nest of squabbling chicks. A calm would fall on the family as everyone turned to the speaker. That's when we settled to hear a tale unroll.

And when the winter breezes drove us indoors we'd sit around a fire in the main hall. Winds whistled round the towers of Marsden Hall, and the fire crackled and the ancient timbers creaked and settled, and someone told a tale from their past.

I liked Great-Uncle George's stories best. He was an old knight and his stories were of wars and daring deeds. Once his huge body must have been strong enough to fight for a whole day in the heavy suit of armour that stands rusting in the gallery of Marsden Hall. "We had to be strong in those days," he said. "We could leap on to a horse's back in full armour. We could run at the enemy and attack him on foot. That's how fit and strong you need to be if you want to be a knight!"

Father talked about the crimes he had come across and the hangings and the villains. Of course Father, as the

Marsden Hall

local magistrate, was hated by everyone in the district. Some magistrates look the other way when a vagrant wanders into their community, but not Father. He sought out the strangers and questioned them. He loved to quote from the Act for the Punishments of Rogues, Vagabonds and Sturdy Beggars that Queen Elizabeth passed in 1597. "You will be taken from here and whipped until you bleed," he said, his eyes fierce and glowing with pleasure at the thought. "Then you will be given a passport to return to the last place where you lived." I still remember how he lowered his voice and added, "And if you ever return to Marsden you will be hanged!" He insisted that my teachers should beat me if I made mistakes in my lessons.

Grandmother had served as a lady-in-waiting to poor Anne Boleyn and knew all about Henry VIII's cruel court and his deadly daughters, Mary and Elizabeth. It was hard for me to believe that she'd once been as beautiful as she claimed. Her face was as smooth and yellow-white as marble; but when you looked really closely you could see that the surface had small cracks in the whiteness and the mask was crumbling like dried clay. As a child I always wanted to reach up and touch it, but I was terrified that her face would disintegrate under my hand and show me the toothless skull beneath. My mother once told me that Grandmother had a sharp tongue. I thought she meant it came to a point like a snake's tail and I watched her closely as she ate to see if it really came to a point. Of course I came to understand that my mother really meant that Grandmother could be harsh and spiteful. But it was hard not to like her.

Grandfather was a soldier in the Scottish wars and terrified us with tales of what would happen if those Border raiders ever crossed the Tyne and reached our Marsden Hall. While Great-Uncle George had grown fat and happy after his days as a fighter, Grandfather shrivelled and grew sour as unripe apples. He hated the things he'd had to do in the wars, he hated the family who spent the money his Marsden estate made ... and he was forever telling us how much he hated the Scots.

Mother served Mary Queen of Scots until she married Father. My mother said little but heard everything and understood it all. When she did finally speak, her words were wise. Father believed that she ran the houshold, organized the servants' work and made sure we were fed regularly and fed well. The truth is she managed the estate for Grandfather and was the axle that the wheel of the family turned around. I just couldn't understand why she ever married my father. But I am glad that she did.

And me? I was expected to train as a knight and fight for some army when I was fifteen. After travelling the world I'd return to take over my father's role as the little emperor of the Marsden estates. I didn't dare tell anyone that I really wanted to go to London to join Mr Shakespeare's acting company and play on the stage. The travelling groups who'd visited Durham and Newcastle had cast a magical spell over me and I could dream of nothing else. So I practised my sword play ... and imagined I was performing on some stage for Queen Elizabeth herself. But that's another story for another time.

On the evening of the "Princes" story that I want to tell you, we were indoors on a wild October evening. We'd supped on roasted capons with an orange sauce. Great-Uncle George had spooned up the last of the sauce, wiped his mouth on his sleeve and pushed away his wooden plate with a look of disgust. "When I was a lad we ate off trenchers of bread," he rumbled. "It soaked up the sauces and you could eat the bread afterwards. That was a meal fit for a knight! You can't eat these wooden platters we have now!"

"When you were a lad the people lived in caves, didn't they?" Grandmother asked.

Great-Uncle George smiled back. "You are like the dewdrop on the end of an old man's nose," he said. "I wish you would drop off."

Granny Marsden's eyes narrowed and her thin hands grasped at a chicken bone. For a moment it looked as if she would throw it.

"When you were a lad the Queen's grandfather was on the throne, wasn't he, Great-Uncle George?" I put in quickly.

Mother had picked up her sewing and gave me a secret smile. I was learning her trick of coming between the battling stepbrother and stepsister and keeping the peace.

Great-Uncle George smiled softly. "Aye, William," he said to me. "When I was born Henry VII was on the throne. The first of the Tudors. The man who saved

England from tearing itself apart in the wars between the York and the Lancaster families."

He rose from the table and walked towards the fire. The rest of the family took their places on the benches and chairs around the fire as they did every night when we stayed indoors. The serving wench gathered the plates and began to carry them off to the kitchen. A chill draught swept through the door as she went out.

The old man picked up a clay pipe from the mantel shelf above the fire and stuck it in his mouth. When Sir Walter Raleigh made tobacco-smoking a new fashion my Great-Uncle George was one of the first to try to copy him. I can still remember the night we gathered round to watch. Somehow the tobacco failed to catch alight, but Great-Uncle George's beard got in the way of the taper and sparked into flame.

Mother was the first to react. She threw a jug of wine in his face. The flames sputtered out and a blackened face looked out through the smoking hair. I can still remember Granny Marsden's hideous cackle that went on and on.

Now Great-Uncle George simply sucked on the cold and unlit pipe. It seemed to comfort him.

That draught caught my neck again and I swung round to see the serving wench slip back into the room and crouch behind my bench. She placed a skinny finger to her lips. The wretched girl wanted to stay in the room and hear a family story!

"Go away, blowse," I hissed. It was an insulting word I'd learned in Newcastle, but, to tell the truth, I wasn't sure what it meant.

Her heart-shaped face was like some wood elf's and her tangled hair must have been combed by using a thorn

bush. "My name's not blowse, it's Meg, Master William," she said quietly.

The girl hadn't been with us long at the time of the Princes' story. I remember her parents had died of the sweating sickness and as an orphan she was taken to my father for a decision on what to do about her. He had been in the gallery of Marsden Hall when the girl had been brought in front of him. She had chestnut hair and sea-green eyes that were as wild as the sea. If she had any grief for her dead parents then she hid it well. "Send her to the almshouse," my father said. "She can pay back the food she'll eat with some hard work in the fields."

"I'll run away," she said.

My father's lip curled with amusement. "You are not allowed to leave the place of your birth without a passport and I will not give you one. You will be whipped and brought back," he explained.

"I'll run away again," she said fiercely.

"You will be brought back again."

"I'll run away again."

"And you will be hanged," my father said. "There is a

gallows tree on the road to the almshouse. Look at it carefully and you'll see what is left of the last person who defied me. He is still swinging there. What's left of him after the crows have finished, that is."

The girl had been about to step forward and do something very unwise when my mother intervened and said to my father, "I have been thinking, James, that we need another serving girl. This one would cost us nothing but the little food that she eats. Why not save the almshouse the trouble?"

"She'll have to be tamed with whippings," my father said.

"I am sure that the girl can be tamed," my mother said gently, and I knew that she'd tame her with kindness.

My father thought for a moment. He was proud that his almshouse was usually empty. The sick were not allowed in until they were practically dead, and beggars were set to work for the farmers on the estate. "Do what you wish, Marion," he sniffed.

So the girl stayed. But if my mother had tamed her, then I couldn't. She didn't understand that a servant's place was not with the family around the fireside.

"Go away … Meg!" I said.

"Or what?" she asked, tilting her head to one side.

"Or I'll call the steward and have you thrown out of the room and out of the house!" I threatened.

She shook her head. "You do *that* and *I'll* tell them what I found in your room when I was changing the sheets."

I felt a cold hand clutch at my heart. For a moment my breathing stopped.

"Get out!" I hissed.

"No," she said. "Does your father know you recite from

books when you tell him you're studying your Latin lessons?"

I looked at her furiously. "They're play scripts," I said, then wished I hadn't told her that. "Just … just don't make a single sound!"

"Wasn't me that started it," she said, settling comfortably just behind me.

I was furious, but there was nothing I could do. Great-Uncle George was standing with his back to the fire and even the dogs had gathered at his feet to listen. "I suppose my story is what you'd call a murder story," he said.

And in the pause I could hear only the crackling logs, the crunching of dogs' teeth on bones and the soft sighing of the wind in the old oak outside.

And at just that moment there came a mighty hammering on the door. The girl jumped and I must admit I almost fell off the bench. My hand flew to the dagger at my belt. Six other pairs of eyes stared wide and wondering in the candlelight. All were turned towards the door.

"I'll answer it," the girl whispered.

Chapter Two

"O, I have passed a miserable night"

The girl stood in the doorway like the steward of the household and announced, "There's a gentleman here to see Sir James Marsden."

Now, Father looks after all the real business of the estate and the house. But Grandfather still sees himself as head of the family when we are all at home. So, as Father rose to his feet, Grandfather jabbed his stick at the girl and said, "Find out who it is. Could be a thief after our gold plate, silver coins and jewels! We let no strangers in here after nightfall!"

Father said, "Ask the gentleman's name, Meg."

But as Meg turned back towards the passage into the hall a cloaked figure fell against her and she was bundled on to the floor. The man practically fell on top of her. She kicked and struggled till she was free, leapt up and raised a bare foot to kick the man in the face.

"Thank you, Meg!" my mother said quietly, her voice carrying over the confused babble from the rest of the family. She turned to me. "William, help the man to a bench at the table."

The man was struggling to rise to his knees. I gripped him under one arm and lifted him. His cloak was cold and smelled of the fresh night air.

Great-Uncle George left the fireside and went round to the stranger's left. Quickly and lightly he slid the man's sword from its loop and threw the weapon, handle first, for Meg to catch. It was all done quickly as he appeared to be helping the man to his feet.

"Thank you, sirs," the man groaned. "Thank you."

Father fussed with a wine jug, threw out the dregs from his own goblet and filled it afresh. As the man sat on a chair and rested his elbows on the table my father pushed the wine to his lips. He drank greedily, let the goblet fall, and breathed deeply.

At last he looked up. I guessed he must be about twenty-five years old. His long dark hair was tangled and he pushed it back from his high, fine brow. The man had straight dark eyebrows over clever eyes and a long nose. Some people might have called him handsome, I suppose. His top lip came down in a small "V" shape in the centre and made him look a little cruel. But that "V" disappeared when he smiled and I wondered if I had imagined it.

"Sorry to burst in on you like this," he said, looking around the family and wondering who he should be talking to. Finally he fixed his gaze on my father. "I believe that I am in a house that is loyal to Her Majesty Queen Elizabeth?"

My father's back was bent with years of grovelling to bishops and greater lords, but it straightened as he replied, "We are Her Majesty's most humble and devoted servants."

The man nodded wearily. "Then I am safe."

"Safe?"

"Safe from Her Majesty's enemies," he explained.

"As safe as if you were in the Tower of London itself!" Great-Uncle George said. "But perhaps you could tell us who you are and how you came here?"

The man looked around the group of serious faces. "You must think I am terribly ill-mannered," he said.

"Ha!" Grandmother sniffed. "George here gives lessons in bad manners. He's spent all his life practising!"

My father glared at her. She glared back. My father turned back to the newcomer. "You look like a gentleman. I am sure there is some good reason for your behaviour."

"Robin Hood looked like a gentleman, and he was a thieving dog!" my grandfather cried. Suddenly he added, "Not that we have anything worth stealing in this house, of course." He slipped his silver goblet under his doublet and his jewelled knife up his sleeve.

Again my father tried to turn our attention back to the stranger. "We are used to these dramas at Marsden Manor," he said grandly. "This ancient house is on the well-worn path between London and Edinburgh. The sights these ancient stones have seen! But these stones tell no tales ... and neither do the Marsden family!"

There was a strangled cough from the doorway as the Meg girl choked back a giggle. I have to admit that the Marsdens tell more tales than Will Shakespeare's theatre company. My father ignored the girl and went on, "Nothing can surprise us, sir. Nothing can shock us. If you are a servant of Her Most Glorious and Radiant Majesty Queen Elizabeth then you are safe here."

"And if you're a Scots spy then you are as safe as a rat in a snake pit," Grandfather added menacingly.

The stranger leaned back and said, "Then I am safe to tell my story to the men of the house."

"Nothing wrong with the women listening," Grandmother said sharply. "Marion here served a queen," she said, nodding towards my mother. "And I served another queen, the sainted Anne Boleyn!"

The stranger's gaze swept the room. "But not your children," he said looking at me and Meg. I hated being called a child and really detested the idea that he mistook Meg for my sister.

I was going to object, but my father squinted in our direction. "Leave us, boy," he said.

I rose slowly and walked towards the door into the hallway. A curtain hung across it to keep out the autumn draughts. As I raised the curtain Meg was beside me. She pushed through, opened the door, then pulled the curtain back across. She put a strong hand on my arm and held me still. Before I could step through the door she slammed it firmly and noisily. We were still in the dining room, but hidden behind the curtain.

The girl pulled my dagger from my belt and made a small slit low in the curtain so we could see into the room as we sat on the floor. "We can't spy on my own family!" I hissed at her.

"Why not?"

"Well … well …"

"*You* can go if you want," she said, and I saw the dark shape of her head nod towards the door behind us.

I said nothing, but pushed my finger through the hole to see what was going on. "I am Humphrey Vere," the stranger was saying. Grandmother had collected some of the food left at the table and was putting it on a plate in front of him and Father refilled his wine goblet. He ate and drank while he talked. "One thing I can tell you and it is no secret … Queen Elizabeth is dying."

There was a muttering from the family and a lot of head shaking. "She's had a long life," my father said.

"A brave lass," my grandmother added, her faded eyes sad and sincere for once.

My mother spoke softly as ever, and to no one in particular, but the others listened when she spoke. "Elizabeth has been a good queen for England, but that doesn't make her a good *woman*," she said. "Don't forget the people who died so she could stay on the throne. Good men like Leicester – good women like Mary Queen of Scots."

My father was breathing so loudly I could hear him from my hiding place. People who repeated stories against Elizabeth had their ears nailed to a pillory. Then, when they'd suffered long enough, the ears were sliced off and the victim set free. But the severed ears were left there as a warning to anyone who wanted to repeat gossip about the Queen. "Yes, Marion," Father spluttered. "But our

guest doesn't want to hear stories about our gracious queen, does he? Master Vere has a story of his own to tell, I'm sure!"

"And a much more important story than an old tale of a murdering Tudor queen," my mother said softly.

"You tell him, Lady Marsden!" Meg gave a whispered cheer in my ear.

"*Thank* you, Marion," my father said loudly as if by shouting he could wipe the dangerous words from the ears of the stranger.

"The Tudors have been harsh, and at times cruel," Humphrey Vere said mildly. "But they have lived through harsh and cruel times! We have needed their strength against the Scots, the French, the Spanish and the Popes."

"Yes," my grandmother's voice cut in sharply. "But there was no need for bullies like King Henry to *enjoy* the cruelty. And, don't forget, he was away in France when we faced a Scots invasion. It was his first wife who organized our defence. A woman *saved* us!" she said triumphantly.

"And a woman's tongue will be the death of us, Mother," said my father. "I've told you before, you cannot repeat these treasons outside the walls of Marsden Hall."

As Grandmother began to reply Great-Uncle George cut in, "But we are being very rude to our visitor. I'm sure he has more important things to do than listen to little family squabbles. Tell us, sir, how can we help you?"

Father turned back to the man and tried to grasp hold of the reins of this conversation. "Yes, Master Vere. You came to us for help?"

"I did," Vere said smoothly as Grandmother subsided into a chair by the hearth and threw a log on to the sparking fire. "I have been trusted with the most important mission in this country since Drake set out to beat the Armada."

"Ahh!" my father sighed. "The succession!"

"Exactly. I have been sent to Scotland to talk to their king, James VI, to see if he is ready to become King James I of England," the stranger said in a low voice, as if the pictures on the walls were listening. "As you know the Queen has no children. And she has always refused to say who will take the throne when she dies."

"That way she has all the hopeful princes and princesses trying to keep her happy with gifts and fine words," Grandmother sniffed. "Crafty little woman."

Humphrey Vere bent his head towards her. "The Queen is skilful in dealing with princes and power," he admitted.

"There are only two people with a chance of winning the English throne," my father said. "Arbella Stuart and James VI, King of Scotland."

"That's right," Humphrey Vere agreed.

"Something has gone wrong?" Great-Uncle George asked.

"It seems my mission was not so secret after all," Humphrey Vere said. "I left York this morning and passed through Durham this afternoon. I had hoped to reach you in time for supper. But when I'd passed through Chester-le-Street it grew dark sooner than I expected. I crossed the Wear and entered the woods on the other side."

"Bournmoor Woods," someone muttered.

"There was a man lying on the ground. He looked dead. I stopped to see if I could help him," Vere went on.

"Ahh! A fatal mistake!" my father cried. "An old trick in these parts. Don't tell me! As you bent over the man he leapt up, dragged you on to the ground and rode off on your horse!"

Vere shook his head. "He took my saddle-bag, but left my purse. He was no ordinary thief. I was dazed, but I heard him ride off. He must have had his own horse waiting."

"So you think he's a *spy*? Trying to intercept the Queen's message to James?" my father asked. He was putting on his magistrate voice, the way he did when he questioned witnesses.

"I'm certain," the visitor said. "And he succeeded. When those messages get into the hands of Arbella Stuart and her followers, they will be able to stir up all sorts of trouble."

"Were they that important?" my father asked.

The stranger took another deep drink of wine and said quietly, "I am just a messenger. I don't know what exactly was in the package of letters to James, but I can guess. There will be questions for him. They will ask 'What would happen to the Catholics if you took over the throne?' If James and his advisers give the right answers then the Queen will leave him the throne."

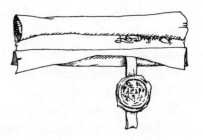

"I don't see why that would be of any use to Arbella Stuart and her friends," Grandmother's harsh voice cut in.

Vere sighed. "There are several possibilities. One is that the thieves can replace the letters with new ones. They could say that Elizabeth wouldn't have James on the throne because he's the son of Mary Queen of Scots. Once the Scottish lords see the English throne slip away from them they'll invade England. If Arbella's supporters drive the Scots back then she'll be England's heroine – remember she's English herself. James will be the villain and Arbella will get the throne."

"I see," Grandmother nodded. "What else?"

"The answers could be forged and sent back to Elizabeth without James ever seeing them!" he explained.

"The *wrong* answers, of course," Great-Uncle George said.

"Of course."

There was a silence in the room as the family thought of the seriousness of the loss. Trouble with Scotland meant extra taxes to pay for armies to fight. But it meant far more to families like us in Durham. The Scots would sweep down through Northumberland before defences could be arranged. They would be at the Tyne within days and at our door shortly after. We could fight them and risk defeat – Marsden Hall would crumble under their cannon and the family would be ruined by deaths or demands for ransom.

On the other hand it was a chance for me to fight. Really fight. It was what I'd been trained for since I was seven years old. And the excitement made me tremble. The girl rested a hand on my arm and felt me shaking. "Don't be afraid," she said.

Afraid! I was angry that she'd misread my shaking, but couldn't argue while we were crouched behind the musty curtain.

"We can't arrange a search tonight," my father said. "The thieves could be anywhere. Tomorrow morning I'll have a messenger sent to the Queen to report the attack on you. You can show us where you were attacked and we can set the hounds on the trail. But tonight you can rest here. Marion," he said to my mother, "call a servant and have a room made ready for our guest ... a fire and a warming pan in fresh sheets." He explained to Master Vere, "The East Wing has a comfortable room. Tomorrow morning we start the search."

The girl thought more quickly than I did. She scrambled to her feet and opened the door. Of course my mother would be coming to call for Meg and it would be difficult to explain why we were crouched there like frightened foxes in their earth.

I crawled after her, closed the door behind me and tumbled down the dark passage into the hall. The door opened and candlelight spilled down the passage. I turned and blinked at my mother. "You weren't listening behind this door, William, were you?" she asked.

"Certainly not, Mother!" I said quite truthfully. "I was just coming to see if our guest needed a room."

"Ahh, good," she smiled. "In the East Tower. Can you tell the steward to arrange it?"

"Of course … and, Mother?"

"Yes?"

"Can I come back into the dining hall now?"

She waved a hand vaguely. "I don't see why not. It's early for bed and your Great-Uncle George was about to tell one of his stories."

I nodded to Meg, who was hiding round the corner. She passed a quick message to the steward and hurried after me back into the dining hall.

The fire had been stirred to a blaze and Great-Uncle George was preparing to launch into one of his tales.

"An honest tale speeds best being plainly told"

"When a king dies there's always trouble! It was always going to be a problem when Elizabeth started to die," Great-Uncle George declared. He stood with his back to the fire, framed by the flames like some devil in a theatre show.

"She won't say who the next ruler of England should be," Grandfather complained. "That would help."

"She refuses," Father explained. "I have heard it from the Bishop of Durham himself." He raised his chin in his self-important way. "I was speaking to him only last week in the cathedral."

"But why does she refuse?" asked Grandmother.

"She says that people will always worship a rising sun and turn their back on the setting sun. As soon as she names her successor she will be abandoned by her people," my father replied.

"People can be cruel like that," my mother said.

Grandmother sniffed loudly. "Aye, I remember our grandfather used to tell us that there is trouble when a king or queen dies. Our grandfather was mixed up in that business when Edward IV died." She looked at me. "That's your great-great-grandfather, Sir Anthony Marsden."

Great-Uncle George glared at her. This was his story and he should be allowed to get on with it. She looked up with a smile as thin as a new moon.

"Anthony Marsden was lord of this manor a hundred and twenty years ago. And Anthony Marsden was swept into the monstrous race to steal the crown of England." He picked up a poker and drew a quick map in the ashes on the hearth. "Edward IV died in London in 1483 ... his son, Edward Prince of Wales, was in Ludlow on the Welsh Border. The dead king's brother, Richard Duke of Gloucester, was at his castle near York. The Prince of Wales set off for London to be crowned ... Richard of Gloucester gathered a small army of his most trusted men and set off to meet him before he got there."

"And Great-Great-Grandfather Anthony Marsden was part of that army?" I asked.

"He was. He was one of Richard's most trusted captains with a band of two dozen hardened fighters from the Marsden estate."

"Two dozen!" I said. "We couldn't find *two* now."

"The estate was so much bigger in those days," my grandfather sighed. "Times change, times change."

Great-Uncle George went on, "All Richard of Gloucester wanted to do was meet the Prince of Wales and see him safely to London ... at least that's what he *said*. Richard of Gloucester wanted to be Protector of the country till little Prince Edward was old enough to run it himself. For Edward was only twelve years old," Great-Uncle George said, looking at me. "Not much younger than you!"

"And our William couldn't run the kitchens in Marsden Manor," my father sneered.

The girl, Meg, giggled and I hid my face in the flame-shadows of my wide collar.

My great-uncle didn't appear to hear her. He went on with Anthony Marsden's story. Let me tell it as my great-great-grandfather told it ...

ANTHONY MARSDEN'S STORY

I gathered a company of mounted soldiers from the estates of Marsden Manor and met Richard of Gloucester at his castle in Middleham. But before we'd had time to rest he set off for London, two hundred miles to the south.

We rode down from the north dressed all in funereal black – after all, the King, his brother, had just died. Townsfolk barred their doors and peasants hid in their haystacks as we cantered through. They needn't have worried. Our lord Richard of Gloucester, Dickon as we called him, wanted friends, not foes, in the country. One of his men-at-arms stole a loaf of bread from a baker's stall. He was hanged from the nearest oak tree and left to dangle as a lesson to the regiments that followed.

I'd spilled blood for Lord Richard and his father in battle and rode proudly at the head of his bodyguard. In those days a man you could trust was worth a battalion of two-faced traitors, as our Dickon was to find out within two years. But that was in the future. Our lord was going to protect Prince Edward, then rule the country for him ... with or without the prince-child's help.

No one ever spoke about Dickon's ambition to take the crown for himself. Everyone knew.

Northampton opened its gates to us, but turned its faces to the ground and hurried about its business nervously. "Where's the Prince of Wales?" my lord Dickon asked, his hand resting lightly on his sword hilt.

The mayor wriggled in his fur-trimmed robes and twisted milk-white, idle hands that were useful only for counting taxes. "Gone, sire, gone."

"When?"

"Yesterday, sire, yesterday."

Dickon sat up in his saddle and sniffed the air as if it disgusted him.

"Which direction? The London Road?" he asked.

"Yes, my lord, the London Road. They should make Stony Stratford by nightfall."

"The Prince is running away from us!" Richard spat. "We'll rest in the tavern tonight and set off at first light to catch the royal worm. That uncle of his, Lord Rivers, wants to control the Prince for himself." His deep eyes looked down the darkening road and he made a decision. "We'll rest here for the night and ride tomorrow at dawn. We should catch them before London. If Rivers gets young Edward safe in the Tower of London then we'll never get him out."

I helped my men find shelter and stabling and joined my lord Dickon at the largest inn on the main street.

But as I was tasting my lord's evening meal of ox tongue with cucumbers, peas and olives to check for poison, a small troop of men clattered over the cobbles of the market square. Dickon went to the window. He had a dagger in his hand.

"Lord Rivers himself," Dickon hissed. "The Prince's uncle. As honest a bucket of toad venom as you could wish to meet. Watch my back!" he ordered as he walked to the door to greet our visitors. Then he turned to the traitor who'd led the Prince away from us and smiled. Oh, Dickon had a wonderful, sweet smile … until you knew what it meant. "Lord Rivers!" he cried. "How good of you to come and meet us!"

Rivers swept off his hat and bowed low. "We had meant to stay here and wait for you," he lied through his serpent teeth. "But the inns here were not good enough, or large enough, for the Prince of Wales."

The inn we were occupying was fit for a king with a pope for his guest. Dickon smiled. "I understand, Lord Rivers," he said. We all understood.

After dinner Rivers was offered rooms in the tavern next door. At midnight, when the candles burned low and the town was left to the street rats, Dickon held a meeting of his captains. He did not need to say much. We were all experienced at hunting the deer and the wild boar. The Prince was just a young deer who was fleeing before us. We'd catch him. "We leave now," he said.

First the doors to Lord Rivers' inn were locked and a company of men left behind to hold him there.

Then a party of scouts were sent ahead to clear the road to Stony Stratford.

Our troops were lined up ready to ride on, although the morning sun hadn't risen and the forest roads were no place to spend the night. An armoured elephant wasn't safe in that country of thieving outlaw rogues.

We rode through that forest like Death's army, almost invisible in our black uniforms and silent apart from the drumming hooves.

We reached Stony Stratford at daybreak and only just in

time. Prince Edward was standing by his pony, ready to ride off, when Richard, Duke of Gloucester, clattered down the street and broke the calm of the spring morning.

The Prince expected to see Lord Rivers. Instead his Uncle Dickon looked down from his war horse at the boy's puzzled face.

There he sat, the mighty soldier, Richard. A thin and pale man with a twist to his shoulder and an arm so withered you'd think he'd never lift that mighty sword. But his eyes told a different story. His eyes burned black and cut to your heart like a Frenchman's knife. You just knew he was the most dangerous man on earth.

"Good day, Your Grace!" he cried when he saw the Prince. "My noble lord!" he said, sweeping his hat from his head in a humble bow. But he was mocking the Prince of Wales, and his soldiers smothered their smiles behind their dusty fists.

"Hello, Uncle Dickon," young Edward said. A serious boy in the way only boys can be serious.

"Now, Your Grace," Richard said, "you are in great danger. You are King of a mighty kingdom."

"I know, Uncle Dickon."

"But there are others who would want to take it from you. Put you out of the way."

"Out of the way?" the wide-eyed boy whispered.

"Out of the way!"

"Which way?" the young Prince asked.

"Death's way," Richard said, and he showed his wolf-toothed grin.

"Lord Rivers will protect us," the Prince of Wales said. "Where is Lord Rivers?"

"Sadly he was one of the men plotting to kill you, Your Grace," Richard of Gloucester cried. "I was forced to arrest him."

"Lord Rivers?" The new King blinked. "He has been my guardian for as long as I can remember. My mother trusts him."

Richard of Gloucester leaned forward in his saddle till the leather creaked. "We believe your mother may be part of the plot to take the kingdom from you. But I am your uncle, your father's brother, and I care for you more than I care for my horse!"

The horse snorted and shifted as Richard pricked it cruelly with his spurs. "More than your horse?" Prince Edward asked.

"More than life itself!" said Richard. Everyone knew that he lied through his teeth. "And so I am going to protect you. I am going to put you behind walls so thick, so high and so well guarded that you'll never get away!"

"Get away!" said the young Prince, wincing.

"Get away?" said Richard of Gloucester. "Did I say get away? Of course I meant get *in*. Your evil enemies will never get *in* to hurt your little body. For there is evil all around us."

The boy looked up to the towering horses and the mud-stained, sun-stained soldiers with their dull steel swords, swords that looked almost as hard and sharp as the men's faces. All he wanted was to be in the safety of Uncle Dickon's fortress. He mounted his pony. He couldn't wait to ride away and lock the door and lock out all the fierce faces and grasping hands that gripped restless reins.

"I'm going to put you in the Tower!" the devious Duke said.

"The Tower, Uncle Dickon?"

"The Tower of London. The home of kings since the great William the Conqueror built it. You'll have the finest apartments with the best food and servants to serve your every want and wish."

The boy gave a soft smile. This was what he'd prayed for. A kindly uncle who'd protect him. A knight as strong and good and brave as Saint George, the dragon-slayer. "Thank you, Uncle Dickon," Edward said politely. Then suddenly he frowned. "But, Uncle Dickon ... didn't my Uncle George die in the Tower?"

The Duke's thin mouth turned down sourly at the thought of his own brother George. At last he said, "He did, he did. George was such a foolish and sad man. Your mother said he plotted against your father and he had to die. It's true poor George said your father was a witch. He even said that *you* should not be king, my lord Edward!"

"Not king!" the boy exclaimed. "Why not?"

"Because your mother had been married before she

married your father. George said a king should not marry a widow."

"Hah!" Edward snorted and looked disgusted at the idea. "Then Uncle George deserved to die. I hope they chopped his head off." He thought about his new home in the Tower and shuddered. "Is the blood still on the floor?"

His uncle gave a short laugh. "No, no. Your Uncle George was given a choice of how he would be executed. He chose to be drowned in a barrel of wine – malmsey wine it was."

"And does his ghost still haunt the Tower?" Prince Edward persisted.

"No, no, no. His ghost was drowned too," his uncle said lightly. "Ghosts can't swim, you know."

The boy nodded and rode on more happily. "I hope I die in my sleep," he said quietly.

"I hope your wish comes true," his Uncle Dickon muttered. He took the pony's reins and turned it away from the rough road towards London where the Prince's mother waited. "And you need not worry about your country, my lord Edward," he said. "Just leave the boring business of ruling it to me. I'll make sure the taxes are collected and the traitors punished. I'll make sure that every man and woman lives in peace – and if they don't I'll string their scrawny necks up from the nearest tree." He looked down on the boy. "For there's nothing so precious as peace, you know."

"I know," young Edward said. "I mean to rule a peaceful country."

"And I'll make sure that you have peace," his uncle said, shrugging his stronger shoulder. "Peace is what you'll get."

He looked across the rolling English fields where peasants stopped their work and watched in silence as the great procession marched its way back to Northampton. "Everlasting peace," he promised, "everlasting peace."

All that day we rode south to London and in every village the people came to see their new king. And they saw him all right. Of course they imagined that the new king would be young Prince Edward. The truth is our Dickon was already plotting to snatch the crown for himself.

And every man in his bodyguard was backing him. It made sense. When the previous king, Edward IV, ruled in London, our Dickon, his brother, had really ruled in the north. Richard of Gloucester kept the troublesome Scots quiet and a lot of the troublesome English in the north too. Every spring there was some new problem to sort out and the men from Marsden estate were there with their bows and swords and pikes to help. Richard of Gloucester was as hard as the iron on his horse's hooves ... and just as crushing if he stepped on you! But he had feelings.

"A weak king only causes trouble in the country. Look

what happened when Henry VI was on the throne,"
he said.

"Civil war!" said the Duke of Buckingham, nodding.
Buckingham was Richard's greatest supporter, but a fat
man planning to make himself fatter with more land and
power. I never trusted Buckingham. As it happened, I was
right. When his time came to die I am only sorry that I
wasn't there to lop off his treacherous head.

The two great lords rode side by side while I was on
Dickon's right hand, watching the woods ahead for outlaws. Not that I expected outlaws to tackle a band of six
hundred armed men!

"My brother Edward IV was a strong king," Richard
went on. "Every one was better off when old Henry VI
died."

I smiled grimly. Old Henry didn't just "die". Old Henry
was murdered. I know, I was there. I carried the bloodied
body of the old fool out of his prison in the Tower of
London. The story went around that our Dickon had
murdered him personally to make the throne safe for his
brother. But that's a slander!

I admit there were deep cuts to Henry's skull. Dickon
said they must have got there as the old King collapsed
and fell. And if Dickon said that's what happened, then
that's what happened. Who am I to call the mighty Duke
of Gloucester a liar?

And now he calmly talked about the death of the Prince
of Wales.

"Prince Edward might die," he said. "Children often die."

"Children die every day," Buckingham agreed sadly.

"Every day. Even princes die," said Dickon.

"Even Princes of Wales die," Buckingham agreed.

"What would happen if the Prince of Wales died?" Dickon asked.

"His little brother, the Duke of York, would become king."

"Imagine that!" my lord cried. "A twelve-year-old boy as king would be bad. A nine-year-old little brother could be a disaster!"

"Unless the little Duke of York died too," Buckingham pointed out.

"Ah, yes. If that ever happened then who would take the throne?"

"Who indeed?" Buckingham sighed. "I suppose the next in line would be yourself, Richard."

"Would it really? I suppose you're right. Well, there's a thing!" he cried. "Of course it would be sad to see the Prince of Wales die."

"Terrible."

"And awful if both Princes were to die."

"Tragic."

"But at least England would have a strong king to defend it against all its enemies."

"There's something good comes out of everything," Buckingham said. "Every cloud has a silver lining, they say."

"Or, in the case of my nephews, the Princes, every silver lining has a cloud!" Richard said, and he roared with laughter.

Our leaders went silent as we rode through a village of filthy, idle peasants who had left their work to watch us ride by. Then Richard turned to me. "The Tower's a safe place for a prince, isn't it, Marsden?" he asked me.

"It wasn't too safe for King Henry VI or your brother, the Duke of Clarence," I reminded him.

The Duke fixed me with his narrow black eyes.

"Accidents happen, even in the safest of homes."

"They do, sire."

"When we get to London I want you to take great care of the Prince of Wales when I put him in the Tower."

"I understand," I said. A cold shudder of fear crawled down my back. I was hoping he wasn't going to ask me to kill the Princes.

"I'm not sure you do, Marsden," he said. "Nothing must happen to the Prince. If he dies then the little Duke of York becomes king. And the Duke of York is with his grasping, greedy, devious mother. It would never do to have a king controlled by Elizabeth Woodville, would it?"

"No, sire."

"So, until the Duke of York joins his big brother in the Tower then no harm must come to this boy," he said sternly.

"And after the Duke of York joins him in the Tower?" I asked.

Richard spurred his horse into a trot. He was eager to reach London and get his hands on the younger Prince. "After?" he called. "Who can tell?"

Great-Uncle George looked around the group, the fire-light shining in his eyes. "The door of the Tower closed safely behind the Prince of Wales. But the horror was only just starting for little Prince Edward," he said.

The whole group were leaning forward to hear what happened next. We were like hunters waiting breathless and silent in the undergrowth waiting for a deer to pass. And sometimes those hunters are surprised by a wild boar crashing behind them. And so we were surprised by the sound behind us.

There was a hammering on the front door loud enough to make the wine jars on the table tremble.

And one word carried through the thick oak doors. The word was, "Murder!"

CHAPTER FOUR

"Is there a murderer here?"

I was the first to reach the door. I lifted the bar and Robyn Smith practically fell into the hallway. He came in with a swirl of rustling leaves and the smell of smoke from his blacksmith forge still clinging to his clothes. He was still wearing his leather apron, stretched like a drum skin over his enormous belly. His grizzled hair was wiry, and his beard thick at the sides but wispy at the front where it was constantly singed away by the heat of the forge.

The huge man looked straight past me to my father. "Murder, Sir James!" he said.

My father gripped the man by his massive arm as a terrier may attempt to grip the leg of a bull, and tried to shake him. "Hush, man, there are ladies here. We don't want to frighten them."

"Sorry, sir," the man rumbled. He allowed himself to be led to the table while I barred the door behind him. The blacksmith's forehead ran with sweat although the evening air had chilled me clean through my velvet doublet.

My father turned to Grandmother and said, "If you would take Marion to the library then I can question the constable here."

Grandmother looked at him with scorn. The white lead powder on her face cracked as she bared her gums.

"Don't be stupid, son. We haven't had a good murder in
these parts since the miller buried his wife on
Framwellgate Moor. I want to hear what the constable
has to say."

Father glared at her, but saw he was going to lose that
battle. He turned back to Robyn Smith and asked, "Now,
Constable, what's this about? Who's been murdered?"

"Oh, I don't know that, sir!" said the blacksmith. The
man was powerful and clever in a sly sort of way. Very
few crimes took place in the village that Constable Smith
didn't know about. But there were always stories that a
little gold could persuade him to turn his head and look
the other way. As a result the rich rogues carried on with
their crime and grew richer while the poor villains were
punished. My father never went into the village if he could
help it, so he never understood how his constable grew fat
on the crimes of others.

"You don't know!" said my father, frowning.

"No, I don't," the blacksmith said, shaking his huge

head slowly.

"I thought you said there's been a murder."

"There has."

"Now you say you don't know who's been murdered."

"I don't."

"So there hasn't been a murder."

"There has."

"So who's been murdered?"

"I don't know!"

My father's face was turning red with rage while the constable's singed eyebrows rose higher into his forehead. "Let's start again, shall we?" my father said. "There has been a murder."

"Yes, sir."

"How do you know?"

"Because John the Shepherd found the body."

"And whose body did John the Shepherd find?"

"I been trying to explain, sir. I don't know."

My father spoke very slowly as if he was talking to a simple child. "Why ... not?"

The constable thought this was a new way of reporting. He spoke just as slowly in reply. "Because ... he ... is ... a ... stranger ... sir."

Grandmother cackled softly and the rest of us tried not to let him see us laughing.

My father sniffed and drew himself up straight. "And where did you find this *stranger*?"

"Hidden under some branches in Bournmoor Woods, sir. A hundred paces west of Widow Atkinson's house. She was gathering herbs when she uncovered the body."

Our visitor, Humphrey Vere, leaned forward suddenly. "Is that where I was robbed earlier this evening?"

"It is," my father said.

"I wonder if there's any connection?" the stranger said.

"I had thought of that myself," my father said stiffly.

"Of course, sir," Vere said, with a small bow of the head.

"Nothing we can do tonight," Father said. "Is the body guarded?"

"Widow Atkinson had some villagers take it into her woodshed to stop the foxes and crows nibbling at him," the smith explained.

"We'll examine the body first thing in the morning. Meet me here after breakfast, Constable Smith," my father ordered. "And bring a few other labourers to help move the body."

"Yes, sir," the smith said. As they made arrangements I felt Meg tugging at the sleeve of my doublet and pulling me towards the door.

"What is it?"

"The body!" she hissed. "We have to look at it!"

"You want to look at a *body*!" I said in disbelief. "Why can't you wait till we have a funeral in the village? I'll arrange for you to have it on the kitchen table if you're that curious."

"You're as stupid as your father," she snapped.

"I'm not!" I said. I dragged her into the hallway so our argument wouldn't be overheard.

She looked at me with her wide green eyes and said, "Sorry, Master William. No one could be *that* stupid."

"Er ..." I was about to argue when she hurried on.

"Look, dead bodies *speak*. They tell you things about their death. But the longer you leave it the fainter their voices become," she said. The girl looked so serious and clever I wondered how she could say such a mad thing.

"Where do you get such ideas?" I demanded.

"I lived in the village until your mother gave me a job here. We have different ways of doing things there. And we all listen to the village wise woman. She even has a way of discovering murderers."

"She's some kind of witch, is she?"

Meg frowned and said, "I don't know about that, but I do know that it works. You write the name of the people you suspect on pieces of paper. Then you fold each paper into a mud ball. The mud balls are dropped into a bucket of water, and the first to unroll as the mud dissolves is the guilty one."

"That's nonsense," I said.

"We could try it in this case," said Meg, "and I'd show you how it works. But we don't *suspect* anyone. And we don't even know who the dead man is till we've looked at him. So let's get to Widow Atkinson's cottage before his voice becomes too faint to hear."

I snatched a cloak from the clothes chest in the hallway, but Meg took my wrist and guided me through the servants' passage to the kitchen and out of the back door.

"If anyone's watching the house then they'll be looking at the front door," she explained.

There was a chill running down my spine and it wasn't just the autumn breeze that stirred the whispering leaves on the stone paths. "Watching? Who'd be watching?"

Meg wore a thin woollen shawl over a black dress which had faded to grey-brown. She didn't seem to feel the cold the way I did. "Someone was watching Humphrey Vere," she reminded me. "And someone saw the robbery, then took revenge on the thief. Maybe he's out there now, watching the house to see what's going to happen next."

We left the gardens through a small gate set in the thick wall. There was only the faintest of light from a quarter moon that kept vanishing behind ragged clouds. There could have been a Scottish army hiding in those shadows, they seemed endless. I didn't like to think what was making the rustling noises in the hedgerows as we picked our way along the wagon way to the village, splashing through puddles in the wheel ruts and scuffing my boots against stones. The barefooted girl didn't seem to notice the problems of the path.

"Widow Atkinson will be able to help us. She's every bit as clever as the wise people who can read. She's clever in her own way," she explained. We passed the first of the cottages. Its shutters were closed and no light spilled out. Villagers went to bed early to save on the cost of candles and fuel.

"What do you mean, 'in her own way'? What way is that?" I asked.

"She's clever with herbs – she reads the weather – she can even tell you where to find something you've lost."

I stopped suddenly. "That's against the law! It's witchcraft!"

She stepped near to me in the dark and said, "Don't use that word. Your father is the local magistrate. He'll have her arrested and ducked in the river to test her. If the ducking doesn't kill her then the cold and the shock will!"

"But if she's a *witch* …" I began.

"I said, don't use that word. Widow Atkinson's a *wise woman*. Witches are people who call on the Devil to help them. Widow Atkinson just uses old country tricks to help us. So don't call her a witch – not to your father– and not to her face!" The girl was fierce and even in the darkness her sea-eyes glowed green. I wondered if she were a cat in human form.

"I wouldn't call her a witch to her face," I muttered. "She'd probably turn me into a hare."

Meg marched on. "No, a hare is quick and beautiful. You're more like a sheep – slow-witted and miserable-faced."

I gripped my knife, wishing I'd brought my sword, and stumbled after her. "You can't talk to the son of the master of the house like that!" I said to her shadowed back.

"We aren't *in* the house now, are we, Master William? We're in *my* world now, so just be grateful I'm helping you."

"How are you helping me?" I asked.

She stopped and turned. "Because this murderer is stirring up trouble for your people. It doesn't matter to us if we're ruled by a Queen Elizabeth, a Queen Arbella, or a King James. We'll still be worked till we're in our graves and taxed by lords who are no better than cutpurses. But it matters to *you* and your family. Because if you gamble on the wrong horse you stand to lose everything."

Meg turned down a narrow footpath off the wagon way and I thought about what she had said. Since Great-Great-Grandfather's day, when the Princes went to the Tower, our family had gambled on a few wrong horses and the Marsden estate was a shadow of the rich manor it had been.

The grassy track led through the edge of the wood to a single-roomed stone cottage with a turf roof. Meg called, "Mrs Atkinson! It's me, Meg Lumley! Can I come and talk to you?"

The door creaked open on ancient hinges and the flickering light of a tallow candle lit the woman's face. I guessed she was as old as my grandmother, but her skin was as fine as good parchment and seemed to glow in the dimly lit room. Her mouth even had a few teeth left in. "Come in, Miss Meg," the widow said. She looked at me with eyes that were a washed-out blue but sparkled in the light of the taper. "Good evening, Master William," she nodded to me.

The house was quite warm inside. A peat fire glowed a dull red in the corner and a pot hung from a metal frame over it. Something smelling like mushrooms and herbs bubbled in there. At the opposite side of the narrow room was a straw bed with sheepskin rugs over it. One wall was fitted with shelves, and the shelves were crowded with bottles and flasks of every shape and colour. There was a small table with a bench behind it, and the old woman nodded for us to sit down. She lowered herself carefully on the bed opposite and watched us.

"You'll have come to see the body," she said.

"We have," Meg said. "You haven't touched it, have you?"

"Why no, Meg Lumley, I know better than that! Bodies *speak*," Widow Atkinson said, echoing the girl's crazy idea.

"And has it spoken to you?" Meg asked.

"It has," the woman said slowly. "But you may hear different things, so I'll not tell you what it said to me till you've looked for yourself. He's in my peat hut."

"Thank you," Meg said.

As we crossed the small garden the scent of a dozen

herbs blew across my face, mixed in my nostrils and hung there like a perfume. Widow Atkinson hobbled alongside us. She had placed the candle in a horn lantern so the night wind wouldn't snuff it out. "That Meg lass will be the next village wise woman after I've gone," she said.

"She will?" I said, startled at the thought.

"Aye. She's a bright one, that lass. You should marry her, Master William!"

"I'm too young to marry!" I said, thinking of the first excuse that came into my head.

"I remember my mother telling me about the Duke of York. He married Anne Mowbray when he was four and she was six years old. She died four years later and he was a widower at eight. Not that it mattered. Some say he was dead a year later himself."

"Which Duke of York was that?" I asked suddenly. "One of the two Princes in the Tower of London?"

"Aye. That was him. Of course some do say he lived on."

"Didn't Richard, Duke of Gloucester, murder both him and his brother Edward?" I asked.

"So you've heard that story, have you?" she asked.

"Part of it," I admitted. "My great-great-grandfather was there."

"A cruel man by all accounts," she said. "But you don't want to believe everything that old fool of a great-uncle tells you."

"So what did happen to the Princes?" I asked.

We reached the door of a small wattle hut, and the woman lifted the latch and opened it. "You'll have to make up your own mind when you've heard the full story," she said. "It's not for the likes of me to go blaming great people like the Marsden family, is it? The

same as you'll have to make up your own mind about what happened to *this* poor man." She led the way into the hut.

The hut was mainly filled with turf, cut into squares and stacked on the floor. The turves made a rough table. On the middle of the faded green top lay the corpse of a man. His hands were neatly folded on his chest and two dull copper coins rested on his lifeless eyelids.

Meg took the lantern, opened its door so a stronger light shone on the body, and began to look at the man from the boots upwards, examining every inch of his clothing.

From where I stood I could see he was about thirty years old, slim but strong-bodied, with straight fair hair brushed back from his forehead. He was wearing riding breeches and long boots. His cloak was long and rich, but rather frayed at the sides. His sword was finest Spanish steel. I'd have loved to own one like that. A leather saddle-bag lay on the floor beside him.

Meg finished looking at him, lifted an arm and let it fall back. She sniffed at the body, then picked up the leather wallet. There were packets of letters inside one of its two pouches. The wax seals, stamped with the royal imprint, had been broken.

Meg looked at Widow Atkinson and said, "It's interesting, isn't it?"

"*Very* interesting," the old woman agreed.

"He travelled a long way on a grey horse. Then, when the horse slowed down in Bournmoor Woods, he was dragged off from behind. He died around nightfall," Meg said.

"You can't know that!" I exploded. "Unless you were there ... or unless you used witchcraft!"

"I told you not to use that word," Meg said crossly. "And there is no magic involved. Simple common sense. Look at the man for yourself. Let the body speak to you."

Widow Atkinson nodded. "I said Meg would make a good wise woman."

I stared at the two women sullenly and walked over to the body. I began studying it as closely as Meg had done. "There's a lot of mud on his boots and his breeches," I said carefully. "But that doesn't mean he's travelled a long way. He could have got that from one river crossing."

Meg spoke quietly while the old woman listened with a faint smile, her eyes half closed. "The mud is of different colours. Red clay, dark loam, light sand, grey dust. You don't find all those soils in Durham. He's travelled from at least as far as York."

"Maybe he's been travelling for a year and never cleaned his boots or breeches," I said.

"If you smell his doublet you'll find his shirt is freshly laundered. You can still scent rosewater. He was a clean man. He wouldn't wear a clean shirt with dirty breeches. No, those breeches were clean this morning – or yesterday – and his boots are polished with beeswax under the mud.

They were cleaned before he left his lodgings too."

"Fine. He's ridden a long way today. But you must have seen the horse. How do you know it's a grey?" I demanded.

"You can't ride a horse without some of its hair rubbing off on to your breeches, or the inside of your sleeve where you rub against its neck."

I picked up the dead arm and looked at the inside of the cuff; the hairs that stuck there were grey or white. "But his death ..." I began. "No! Don't tell me. Let me guess." Meg and the old woman waited patiently. "His sword ... it's in its loop and it's not stained with blood or even notched where it's struck another sword. So he never had time to draw his sword." The woman nodded. "But are you sure he was attacked from behind?" I asked. They didn't reply, but left me to work it out.

I looked at his cloak. It was fastened with a cord at the neck. On his throat the cord had left a purple stripe. "He was strangled with his own cloak. Someone pulled it from behind and kept pulling until he was dead?"

"Good," Widow Atkinson murmured.

"And killed in Bournmoor Woods?" I looked at the cloak and the boots. "He was found on the edge of the woods under a pile of branches. The backs of his boots are scuffed as if he was dragged backwards off the path – and his cloak has picked up leaf mould. But it isn't in a *terrible* state, so he can't have been dragged far."

"And we may even be able to find the tracks of his heels tomorrow in the daylight if your father and his constables don't go trampling over the paths," Meg suggested.

"So, how do you know he died at nightfall?" I asked.

"I've seen lots of bodies," Widow Atkinson said. "I've watched them die and washed them ready for burial. And when a body dies it always does the same thing. It goes stiff about five hours after death. Lift his hand. See – it's just starting to go stiff now. He was alive this afternoon – he was dead by nightfall. He died somewhere in between. His light went out as the sun went down."

I looked at the women with new respect, but couldn't resist teasing them. "The body has spoken and told you all that. Now all you have to do is tell me who killed him ... and why?"

"That's your father's job," Meg said with a shrug. "He's the magistrate."

"You won't help any more?"

"Tomorrow. When it's light, I may," she said. "But perhaps you could learn something by looking at his saddlebag. He has clothes in one bag – he has these letters in the other."

"You haven't read them?" I asked the widow.

"Hah! Lad, I can't read! Who'd teach a peasant woman to read? No, I can hear what the body has to tell me. You can read what those letters have to say."

"They are addressed to King James himself! I can't read the King's letters!"

"Why not?" asked Meg. "Someone else has read them."

I decided quickly, pushed the bag with the letters under my cloak and said, "I'll take them back to the house where there's better light."

Meg opened the door for me. "I'll guide you back, Master William," she said.

"You're too kind," I said tartly.

"No, I'm not. I want to hear what's in those letters."

"They may be secret!" I objected. "I can't read them to you!"

"Then I can't guide you back," she grinned. "You'll probably die when you fall into a ditch – or the murderer may still be out there looking for the letters – or the spirits may be walking in the graveyard at this hour. Good luck, Master William!"

The moon disappeared behind another cloud and I couldn't even find my way to the front gate in that light. "Oh, come along. I'll read the letters to you," I said.

"I thought you might," she replied, and we slipped into the night that was dark as a grave.

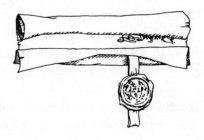

CHAPTER FIVE

"Thou art a traitor: off with his head!"

I hid the saddle-bag in the chest in the hall when I put my cloak away. Meg and I crept back into the dining hall where Great-Uncle George was still standing in front of the fire.

The stranger, Humphrey Vere, had gone to bed, but the family was happy to sit there and listen to my great-uncle talking. Father played chess with Grandfather and seemed to be studying the game, Mother was sewing and Grandmother appeared to be dozing, but I knew they were all listening.

It seemed that, after the disturbance of our visitor, the old knight was settling back into the story of the Princes in the Tower as his grandfather had told it to him ...

"How did Richard of Gloucester kill the Prince of Wales?" I asked. My throat felt dry and my eyes were damp.

"Not so fast, my boy, not so fast. There are worse things than facing your death in the darkness of the Tower."

"What's worse than that!" a voice cried softly. No one noticed that it came from the serving girl, who had no right to be there anyway.

My great-uncle just answered, "It's worse to watch the death of someone else."

We arrived in the great bustling dirty city of London with Lord Richard and the Prince of Wales. The people didn't know whether to cheer the Prince or hide from his black-cloaked bodyguard. When they heard our voices and knew we were from the north they decided to hide.

Now, one prince was no use to us without the other prince. But the Prince of Wales' mother fled into the safety of Westminster Palace with her younger son, the little Duke of York. My lord Dickon's face was as black as his suit with rage when he heard. "They say she's a witch," he hissed. "Perhaps we'll get to hang her as a witch some day ... but not until we have the Duke of York in our gentle hands."

Richard started giving orders in the name of the young king-to-be. But the Prince still had his supporters. Honest men like Lord Hastings. But this is not a world for honest men to live in. It's a world where honest men die!

Lord Hastings started to wonder if the Prince would ever be crowned. Imagine that! Our Dickon had said the Prince would be crowned. "Lord Hastings is calling me a liar!" my lord Dickon said. "His tongue wouldn't wag so stupidly if his head were removed from his body."

"That's true," I said. I felt a tightness around my throat that made it hard to swallow.

So my lord Richard set a trap. He invited Hastings to a meeting in the Tower. We were in the great hall with its gold-threaded tapestries glinting in the rainbow light from the stained-glass windows.

Richard was sitting down to dinner. But as I moved behind to follow him into the room he said, "No dinner for you today, Marsden. I have a little task for you. If you do it well I may let you eat."

Then he gave me secret instructions and sent me to gather a group of the best six armed men in our garrison. Naturally I chose the men of Marsden Manor. They would murder their own mothers if I told them to – and they would murder me if someone paid them enough money. Loyal men. Honest men. Vicious men.

The smell of the roast swan was making my mouth water and my stomach gurgle as I hid behind the tapestry at an open door.

I peered out to see Richard and the Prince at the high table, dabbling their fingers in rosewater and waiting to be served. Then I saw Lord Hastings arrive and gave a silent signal for my men to stand ready. As Hastings bowed before our Dickon, the Duke jumped to his feet in a fit of rage.

"Treason!" Duke Richard cried. "This man Hastings is plotting against the King! I have secret information that tells me he is a traitor! Call for my bodyguard."

And that cry was a sign for us to rush into the room and snatch the bewildered Hastings. Richard of Gloucester shouted, "By St Paul, I will not eat my dinner till I see his head off!"

Some of the Prince's supporters began to snatch at their swords. We all knew what we had to do. I headed for Lord Stanley. My own sword was already raised and I struck him over the head with the flat of the blade. He fell under the trampling feet of the confused diners. I put my boot under him and rolled him safely under the table. I'm thoughtful like that.

Buckingham's men dragged Lord Hastings out of the

meeting room in the Tower and on to the green outside. I snatched the Prince of Wales and held him to stop any rescue attempt. But most people were too busy hurrying to the windows to look at the scene.

"What's happened to Hastings?" the boy cried.

"He was plotting to kill you, sire," I explained.

"But what will they do to him?"

"They'll do what they do to all traitors," I said.

The young Prince was grey as a summer rain cloud and he held a small hand to his mouth as if he wanted to vomit. "I want to watch," he said. He struggled towards the group at the window who had suddenly gone silent.

We were watching from the windows as Buckingham's men searched for a block and an axe. They never found them. Dickon's instructions had come too late for us to get the execution equipment from the armoury.

But they did find wood that was laid out ready to repair the Tower. The soldiers roughly laid Hastings' head across a plank, and even as he said his prayers a man in a black cloak and black mask stepped from the Garden Tower. He

carried a two-handed war sword. The unknown man was too tall and lean to be the usual Tower executioner. And he was too rich. I could make out that the spurs on his boots glittered a rich gold.

Hastings was sent to meet our maker with a single sweeping stroke of that sword. There was a sigh from the watchers as if they had been holding their breath since Hastings was dragged from the room.

What was the young Prince thinking as he watched that bloody scene? Was he afraid that the king-to-be was now a corpse-to-be?

Oh, but the Tower is like a man with two faces. One is cheerful and handsome, the other is ugly and cruel.

Of course, Prince Edward had only ever seen the handsome face of the Tower. We'd put him in the royal apartments with their windows of coloured glass and wall hangings with gold and vermilion pictures of angels and birds. Even the floors were fit for a king to walk on with their tiles decorated with leopards and deer. The only thing he missed was company. So now we set about getting him his little brother to play with.

For some reason the Queen, his mother, didn't want to give up the Duke of York to our Dickon. "It's as if she did-n't trust me," the Duke of Gloucester said. I could tell the Queen had hurt his feelings. She was living across the river from the Tower in Westminster Palace with her younger son.

"We could go in and drag her out," I said one day as we looked down from the lime-washed walls of the White Tower to her hideaway.

The Duke frowned at me. "I'm not a violent man, Marsden! You know me! No, no, no! We'll give her a chance to hand over the little brat quietly. After all, the Prince of Wales may be crowned king some day soon. She can't stop his brother going to the coronation!"

"Wouldn't be right, that, sire," I agreed.

"So let's pay her a visit in Westminster Palace," he said.

"Should we take an armed guard, sire?" I asked.

Dickon looked at me sadly. I could tell he was disappointed in me. I'll swear I almost blushed. "Marsden," he sighed, "we will not take an armed guard – we don't want to frighten the woman." Then his face changed to a grin as evil as a gargoyle carved on Durham Cathedral gutters. "We will take an army and terrify her!"

I laughed uneasily. "So we will drag her out if she refuses?"

"No, Marsden. We will not have to use our army."

"Why not?"

He reached to his belt and snatched a dagger. In an instant it was at my throat. "You see this dagger, Marsden?"

"Yes, sire," I said. My voice did not seem to be as strong as I'd have liked.

"I am holding this dagger at your throat."

"Yes, sire."

"I am not going to use this dagger to cut your throat!"

"I am pleased, sire."

"But I would like you to hand over your son to me. Will you do that, Marsden?"

"Of course, sire!" I gasped. Then I realized I didn't have a son.

Richard put the knife away and said, "You see? I didn't have to threaten you with the knife, it just happened to be there in my hand – and I don't have to threaten the widowed Queen with an army. It will just happen to be surrounding her safe little nest in Westminster. I don't want people saying that I threatened or bullied my dead brother's wife, do I?"

"No, sire."

"Shall we see if she hands over her son?"

"Yes, sire."

"Then organize a bodyguard of around a thousand men. I will persuade the Archbishop of Canterbury to talk to the Queen. She'll listen to him. She'll trust him, and believe him if he says the little Duke of York will be safe in the Tower with the Prince of Wales."

"But will the Archbishop do it?"

Dickon fingered his dagger again and I stepped back nervously. "Would you do it, Marsden?" he asked mildly.

I swallowed hard, imagining the tip of that dagger pressed to my throat. "I'd do it, sire," I told him.

"Then arrange that bodyguard to meet me at the Tower tomorrow morning. Leave the Archbishop to me."

And so the next day we marched across the river Thames to ask the Queen to hand over her nine-year-old son. What would you have done if you'd been the Queen?

My great-uncle paused in his story. It was all part of the Marsden storytelling custom. From time to time the storyteller would stop and put the listeners in the shoes of the people from the past.

My mother looked up from her sewing and said, "A thousand Archbishops of Canterbury wouldn't get my William from my protection." She smiled at me.

"No," Grandmother mumbled from her chair by the

fire. "But a thousand soldiers with swords might. Anyway, it's not as if the Duke of York was her only son. She had the Prince of Wales and half a dozen daughters."

My mother didn't argue, but said, "The Prince of Wales was already in Richard's clutches. Once he had the Duke of York they were both as good as dead. As long as she had the Duke in Westminster then both boys were safe. There must have been another reason why she handed him over."

"Hah!" My grandmother laughed harshly. "The Queen wasn't interested in saving her sons' lives. She was only interested in saving her own miserable neck. Richard could kill the *boys*, but he didn't need to kill *her*."

My mother nodded. "I think you may be right, Mother-in-Law. That's why I say, the Archbishop could persuade her, and Richard of Gloucester could bully her, but I wouldn't hand over my son. Because I value my son's life more than my own."

"No wonder he's spoilt," Grandfather grated from his seat at the chessboard. "I'd hand the boy over."

"Me too," my father agreed.

"Thanks very much," I said bitterly. I wondered whether the nine-year-old Duke of York felt as bitter when his mother handed him over to his Uncle Dickon. Probably not – after all, he didn't know what was coming.

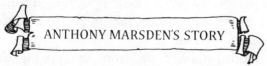

ANTHONY MARSDEN'S STORY

Of course Elizabeth handed over the young Prince to Richard and now he was ready to complete his plan.

First the lies ... and then the executions.

All the lords of the land had gathered in London for a coronation. My lord Dickon called them together in a parliament.

"My lords!" he told the parliament, "I have called you here today with some sad and painful news."

Their lordships were dressed in their finest silks and velvets to meet Richard of Gloucester, the Protector, at Baynard's Palace. Some looked sullen and hostile as if they knew what was coming. None looked angry enough or foolish enough to argue with him. The Duke of Buckingham stood behind Dickon and made all the right replies to the Protector's speech.

"Yesterday I had a visit from Bishop Stillington, the Bishop of Bath and Wells."

It was true! The weedy, snivelling, little toad-wart had visited Richard and bowed low enough to wipe his boots with his hat.

"Bishop Stillington had some dreadful news. A secret that he has kept for over twenty years. A secret that must be revealed now before we go ahead with the coronation of young Edward. You see, Bishop Stillington told me that King Edward IV, my dead brother, was in love with a certain Lady Eleanor Butler. In fact he was so in love with her that he offered to marry her. As you know, an offer of marriage is as serious as a wedding service."

Several of the lords began muttering to one another. They could see where this was leading. "As a result," Richard went on, "King Edward was not free to marry the present Queen, so his children, the Princes in my care, can never become kings of our country!"

"Then who is the heir to the throne?" Buckingham cried – as if everyone in the hall didn't know.

Richard raised a crooked shoulder. "My brother George of Clarence has a son ... but George of Clarence was executed as a traitor and, as we all know, a traitor's son cannot take the throne."

"Then you, Richard of Gloucester, must be our king!" Buckingham shouted. Some of the lords who saw which way the wind was blowing began to shout for Richard too.

Richard raised a hand. "I love my country – but I am not fit to take my brother's crown," he said.

"You *are*!" some lords yelled and others joined in the cries.

"I could not even consider taking the crown ..." Richard began, but his voice was drowned by the uproar in the hall. He raised a hand and waited for the noise to drop. "I could not consider taking the crown of England ... unless it was the wish of all the great lords present here today."

He swung round, marched off the platform at the end of the hall and I followed him into the room behind. "Well?" he asked sharply.

"A great performance, sire," I said.

"And what will they do?"

I pretended to think of this for a while as the shouting and the excited babble from the hall carried through the door. "Well ... they could vote for you to be King Richard III ..."

"Or?"

"Or we can kill them," I said.

Richard pulled a pained face. "Marsden! Always thinking of killing! I am a kind man and hate the sight of blood, as you know. Send messages to the north and arrange for an army of about five thousand men to come down to London for my coronation."

I grinned. "The Londoners hate us northerners, sire. They think we're wild and savage."

"I am a northerner and I'm not savage," he said. "And, while I remember, Earl Rivers is still our prisoner at Sheriff Hutton Castle, isn't he?"

"Yes, sire."

"When you send messages north for an army, send a message to Sheriff Hutton Castle. Tell Ratcliffe to take Rivers to Pontefract and execute him."

"Any particular charge, sire?" I asked.

"Plotting to kill me," Richard said. His grin was sharp-toothed as a ferret. He had Rivers' head knocked off with as much thought as a boy knocks an apple off a tree.

That was when a messenger came into the room and said, "Their lordships would like to talk to you, sire."

Richard placed his dark-blue velvet hat on his head and walked slowly back into the hall. It was silent now and the men hid their feelings behind faces of carved alabaster.

The Duke of Buckingham stepped forward, bowed low before our Richard and spoke in a voice loud enough to carry to the rafters of the hall.

"Richard, Duke of Gloucester, I have been given the humble duty of presenting a request to you by the parliament met here today. We have decided, without exception, that you should be offered the throne of England. That you are the true heir to your late brother's kingdom and are the only man who can keep the peace."

"But is this the wish of the people, as well as of these noble lords?" Richard asked.

"Aye!" came mutterings from the lords.

Dickon twisted his hands and looked up to the heavens – I was sure there were a few of his victims looking down with some very unheavenly feelings. "I have no wish to take on the cares and the weights of kingship," he said. No one believed him. "But I have a duty to my people. God has given me this duty. I cannot turn my back on the will of God. I humbly accept."

"God save the King!" the Duke of Buckingham cried and threw his hat in the air.

"God save the King!" came the echoes of the lords. But some caps flew higher than others and some hearts sank.

Richard turned his back on the gathering and winked at me.

I hurried about my bloody business. I was surprised at how little blood we'd had to shed to place our little Dickon on his brother's throne. But I knew that more would have to flow to keep him there.

My Great-Uncle George paused again. "As I say, when a king dies it is a desperate and a dangerous time."

My grandmother nodded. "The old Queen isn't even dead yet, and the deaths have started."

"Have they?" my father asked, looking up from the chessboard and blinking.

Grandmother leaned forward and gripped her ebony-wood cane with the silver handle. She pulled herself to her feet. "There is a body lying in Widow Atkinson's cottage, and if that is not linked to the dying Queen then my head is thicker than Constable Smith's hammer." She pointed the stick at my father. "You're the magistrate. It's up to you to get to the bottom of this mystery. If the killer isn't caught and punished then there'll be more bloodshed before the winter's done," she promised. "I'm going to bed!" It was the signal for us all to go to bed, even though Great-Uncle George's story was unfinished.

Meg leapt to her feet and opened the door for Grandmother. She hurried ahead to make sure the warming pan was in place in the bed and the jakes had been emptied in case the old woman wanted a pee in the night.

Life went on. And the body of a stranger in Widow Atkinson's peat hut grew colder. Tomorrow I would help my father solve the mystery. But first I had to study the documents the man had stolen.

CHAPTER SIX

"It is now dead midnight"

I placed three candles by my bedside, spread the papers on the top of the bed and reached for one. The soft tapping on the door made me guiltily throw the covers over the papers.

"Who's there?"

"Meg."

"What do you want?"

"You said you'd read the papers to me," she said. "Can I come in?"

"No! Go away."

There was silence. That had put her in her place, I decided. I uncovered the documents and leaned forward. "Interesting?" she asked.

I think I jumped higher and faster than a startled stag. "What? You ... what are you ... I thought I told you to go away!"

She folded her arms and looked at me. "Master William, you have letters from the Queen of England to the King of Scotland. Reading them is probably *treason*. And for treason you are not just executed – you are hanged, drawn and quartered."

"I know that ..."

"And that means you are hanged by the neck until you

are almost … but not quite … strangled. Then you are cut down and stretched on a butcher's table. A knife is inserted into your belly and a long cut is made."

"Yes, I've heard about all that," I said. I could almost feel the knife entering me. The girl didn't stop.

"Your guts are taken out and thrown on to a charcoal brazier at your side so you can hear them sizzling. And finally, your treacherous head is cut off and stuck on a pole so all the world can see just what happens to a traitor."

"I'm not a traitor," I said.

She gave her sweetest smile and said, "Tell that to the Queen. Because she'll find out about this and she'll be furious."

"She won't find out."

"She will!"

"How?"

"I'll tell on you."

"But you helped me take them away!" I wailed.

She just smiled and said, "Sizzle! Sizzle!"

"You're a witch!" I said.

"And you're a traitor. Sizzle! Sizzle!"

Of course I wasn't really frightened by her threats. But she could cause me a little trouble, so I said, "It won't do any harm to read the documents to you."

"No harm at all. They can only hang, draw and quarter you once. They can't make it any worse just because you read the letters to a serving girl."

"Stop going on about hanging," I snapped.

"Sorry, Master William," she said, and sat on the bed so heavily the papers scattered.

I picked them up and studied them. After a minute she

became bored. "I thought they taught you how to read," she said.

"The letters are in Latin," I said. "I have to read them and then translate them into English."

"You must be really clever," she said.

"Quite," I said modestly.

"Strange that you don't look it," she said.

I turned back to the letters and worked on them for five more minutes before I was ready to share their meaning with her. I looked up. She stretched out on my bed, rested her chin on her hands and listened. "The Queen doesn't believe she's dying," I said. "She says the rumours about her health are wrong. But she is interested in knowing what will happen to her kingdom. It seems that what she wants is some word from James about how he would rule … if he were selected. But she doesn't exactly say, 'What would you do?' It's not that simple."

"*She* wants to tell *him* how to rule," Meg said.

I blinked. "How did you know that, witch?"

She lowered her head and looked at me from under her dark eyebrows. "Don't even say that in fun, William."

I suppose I hadn't understood until then how important it was to her. "I won't," I promised.

She took a deep breath. "It's all about death," she explained. "The Queen doesn't want to die. That's why she wears all that make-up, they say, and why she wears ridiculous red wigs. She wants to stay young forever."

"She has a wizard friend called John Dee," I remembered. "He's been experimenting for years to find the secret of everlasting life."

Meg nodded. "Good Christians die and go to Heaven. She must have been a very wicked woman to be so afraid of dying."

"But what has this to do with the letters?"

"Ah! Elizabeth wants James to take over the country and run it exactly as she has run it for fifty years. Nothing will change. In that way it will be as if she were still alive. She can't bear the thought of England changing after she's dead."

"That's pretty much what it says in the letter. She tells him to keep persecuting the Catholics, to keep attacking the Spanish at sea and never to trust the French. She wants him to keep the English wool trade strong and keep the great lords weak and powerless."

"They won't like that," Meg said quickly. "Just imagine it! Some earls and dukes have been waiting years for her to die so they can really grab power and wealth. If they find out King James is going to be as bad as Queen Elizabeth, there's no telling what they'll do!"

"They might join together to stop him coming to England," I said. "There'd be a war to keep James and the Scots out."

"And we know who'll be in the front line of any battle against the Scots," Meg said. She looked at me.

"Somebody has read these letters. We have to find out who … and we have to stop them spreading the word! First we hide these packets of letters somewhere in your room."

"We could give them back to Humphrey Vere," I suggested.

"Not till we're sure about him," she said.

"What do you mean?"

"I mean … I don't trust him any more than I trust Constable Smith or his night watch."

"Constable Smith!"

"Trust nobody, William," she said earnestly.

"Fine." I took the packets and opened a small split in the feather mattress. Goose down floated in the candle-light as I stuffed the letters in. "But I can't hide the sad-dle-bag in there," I said.

The girl took it from me, wiped the grey horse hair from the inside and frowned. She looked for a moment as if she were going to say something, then changed her mind. "We'll put the pouch back with the body, first thing in the morning. I'll wake you at daybreak," she said. "Then we'll go in search of the killer."

"Where do we start?" I asked.

"By looking for a grey horse!" she said.

"But why?"

She sat on the end of the bed and looked at me silently. I knew what that meant – work it out, William.

"The murdered man waited in the entrance to Bournmoor Woods," I said. "As evening fell he attacked Humphrey Vere and stole the saddle-bag from him. He ran off to where his grey horse was waiting and mounted it. But, before he'd come out of this side of the woods, he was dragged from his horse, strangled and ... and not robbed."

"But he *was* robbed," Meg said.

"He *was*," I agreed. "He was robbed of his horse! A thief would have gone through his saddle-bag and looked for valuables. He'd have broken open the seals on the letters to see if there was any money inside. But he would have left the letters behind because they're worthless."

"Good," Meg said approvingly.

"So Grandmother's wrong. The murder *wasn't* to do with the Queen ... it was simply a horse thief. A good horse is worth ten golden guineas. The letters are worthless ... to a horse thief. Where do we start looking for a horse thief?" I asked.

Meg said, "In the village, of course. We'll start there in the morning. There aren't that many stables where you could hide a strange horse. Especially a good grey that can travel the length of the country."

"Brilliant!" I said.

"Thank you," she smiled as she walked to the door.

"What?" I said.

"Thank you for saying I'm brilliant!"

I frowned. "Not you ... *me*! After all, I worked it out!"

She closed the door much harder than she needed to. The scowl on her face would have turned cream sour.

I waited till she was out of earshot before I let out my laughter.

I woke from the dream of a knight on a white horse. I was raising my sword to meet his charge, but I froze. There was something wrong with his horse. Something wrong with its colour. I was so worried about it I lowered my sword and felt the punch of the lance on my shoulder.

I gave a cry of pain and my eyes flew open. Meg was waking me with a sharp-knuckle punch to the shoulder. In the slate-grey light of the early morning her tangled hair looked wilder than ever. "I'll be with you in ten minutes," I said wearily.

"Ten minutes!" she said. "It doesn't take you ten minutes to get out of bed!"

"I need to wash and comb my hair," I hissed. "Get out."

"Your hair doesn't need combing. It's neat enough."

"I need to comb it to get the lice out," I reminded her. "Maybe they don't bother you," I added.

"They don't," she smiled. "Widow Atkinson gives me herb lotion to keep them off. Shall I ask her to give you some now?"

"Go away. I want to get dressed," I said.

She sighed. "You men take so long to get dressed. Lacing up your hose and fastening your doublet. Why can't you just throw a dress over your head like a woman?"

"Because I'd look pretty stupid in a dress. Get out!"

She pulled a face and bounced across to the door. "Five minutes, William," she said.

As I pulled on my boots I wondered when she'd stopped calling me "Master"and if I should make her start again. I decided it probably wasn't worth the trouble.

I grabbed the saddle-bag and stepped into the corridor. Every floorboard and stair of the old house seemed to creak as I walked along the landing and down the stairs. Sweat on my brow cooled as I stepped into the fresh morning air which was as chill as a steel sword.

At least I was able to see my way to Widow Atkinson's cottage this time. A faint wisp of smoke was coming from her chimney, but we didn't disturb her as we left the empty

leather pouch by the body in the hut and hurried out.

We headed straight for Bournmoor Woods and reached them as the sun rose and gave us enough light to see the marks on the path. There were prints of bare feet, boots, horse's hooves and sheep hooves. About a hundred paces in we found a place where the ground was trampled by the side of the path and where footprints led into the undergrowth.

"Walk very slowly down the path," Meg ordered.

I did as she said. She looked towards me and shook her head. "It's not an easy place to hide," she told me. "No wide trees close to the path to hide behind. Why didn't the killer wait in the middle of the woods where the big oaks are? A horse thief can hide behind a trunk or even in the branches and drop down. There are still enough leaves on the branches to hide a man."

I reached Meg and looked at the flattened undergrowth. "You can see where the body was dragged through the bushes," I said.

The girl nodded. She stopped and pulled a leaf from a small plant, rubbed it between the palms of her hands and sniffed at it. "This is the patch of wild herbs Widow

Atkinson was collecting from when she came across the body. If she hadn't been here yesterday evening, he could have stayed hidden for days. The horse thief must have gambled that it would be a while before the body was found. He could have been as far away as London if he had had a week."

"But he *didn't*," I said. "So he may still be in the district."

We walked back to the path. Meg stared down it again. "If the thief didn't hide behind a tree, then he just stood here and waited."

"If I saw a man standing in the middle of the path, I'd draw my sword. It's only natural," I said.

"Would you?" she challenged.

"Of course! I wouldn't just ride up to a horse thief and let him pull me down and murder me!"

"How would you know he was a horse thief?" she asked.

"Well ... he'd look like one," I said weakly.

"You mean he'd look like a poor peasant. He'd look like my friends in the village?"

"Yes," I said.

She suddenly stepped towards me, her face dark and fierce. "Thank *you*, Master William. That's the sort of thing you *would* think. Not all poor people are rogues – and not all you rich people are honest!"

She turned on her heel and marched away. "What I meant was ..." I began.

"I hope he gets you next," she said, throwing the words over her shoulder. "And I hope he turns out to be as well dressed as you."

I was running to keep up with her. "Of course, you're right, Meg," I said. "We have to find the murderer."

"Find him yourself," she snapped and kept striding down

the path, her wild hair flying in the light morning breeze.

"I need your help!" I said. "You're the only one who can talk to the villagers."

"I don't think one of them did it!" she said.

"That's what I mean. You can prove your friends innocent."

She stopped so suddenly I ran into her back. If her stare had been a green flame then I would have been burned to a cinder.

She pointed a bony finger with a ragged nail at me. "But you're the one who can read the papers and talk to the people in your house."

"Exactly!" I cried. "We need one another."

She walked on a little more slowly. "Very well. I have to serve breakfast soon. But after breakfast we'll go and talk to Walter Grey. If anyone knows where a stolen horse might be then Wat Grey will."

"Is he a horse thief?"

She turned down the corners of her small mouth. "He's a horse dealer ... but he doesn't always ask too many questions about where the horses come from. You understand?"

"Oh, yes," I grinned. "What you're trying to say is ... he's a horse thief!"

She twisted her face into a mockery of a smile. "At least he's not a murderer like your great-great-grandfather."

She felt she'd had the last word and there was a spring in her step as she hurried back to Marsden Manor.

CHAPTER SEVEN

"Think on the Tower; despair and die"

The family were still in their rooms when I returned, but our guest, Humphrey Vere, was sitting at the hall window and looking out on to the garden with its yellowing leaves and faded pink roses.

"Good morning, William," he said. "You are out early."

His pale eyes seemed to be looking through me. I couldn't meet his gaze. I felt that if I looked him in the eye, he would know that I'd read his letters and where they were hidden. I could not begin to explain that, and I didn't want to have the story dragged out of me with red-hot pincers as I lay stretched on a rack in the Tower.

"I've been to the woods … looking at the spot where the man was killed."

"Ah!" he nodded eagerly. "And did you find anything interesting there?"

"It's what I *didn't* find," I told him. "I couldn't see why he was attacked in that spot. There's a tangle of undergrowth at the side of the path, but no real hiding place for a thief."

"Perhaps the thief wasn't hiding. Perhaps he stood in the path."

"I thought of that," I said. "But he'd have drawn his sword."

"How do you know he didn't?" Humphrey Vere asked.

Suddenly I saw I had dug myself a trap and was about to throw myself into it. "Er ... a man on a horse with a sword would beat a man on foot," I said.

"And what if the killer was on horseback?" he asked.

I hadn't thought of that. But it was a good idea.

"So, why did you go?" he asked.

"Just curious," I said.

"It's good to see a lad with a bit of curiosity. You must get bored around here."

"Sometimes," I admitted. "I do weapons training most days, but it's not real practice chopping at a post with a blunt-edged sword."

"I agree. Maybe we can have a contest – blunted swords, of course. Before I leave in a day or two."

The idea was thrilling. "Would you really?"

"Of course," he smiled. "I'll go and look at this murdered man this morning – see if it's the one who robbed me – and, I hope, collect my saddle-bag and letters."

I turned away quickly before he could see the confusion and guilt on my face. "Can I get a servant to bring you breakfast?" I asked.

"That's good of you," he said.

When I returned with Meg and breakfast, Great-Uncle George had come downstairs and was talking to our guest at the window seat. Meg put the food down and lingered there to hear my great-uncle talk.

"You say you serve at the Queen's court, Master Vere?" the old man was asking.

"I am a captain of the garrison at the Tower. I'm loosely attached to the royal bodyguard ... but I do special duties." The stranger spread his hands in apology. "I'm sorry, I'm not free to say what they are!"

"Of course not! Of course not!" Great-Uncle George said quickly. "My own grandfather had a similar job with Richard III. I was just telling the family last night about the Princes in the Tower."

"A terrible mystery," Vere said.

"Indeed! Even my grandfather was puzzled by the disappearance of the Princes ... and he was *there* when they went missing!"

The old man leaned back against the stone frame to the window, looked out on to the garden and remembered ...

ANTHONY MARSDEN'S STORY

Dickon was a busy man. The new King had to talk to all the lords and see for himself just how loyal they were, see if they had any objections to his being crowned instead of young Edward, Prince of Wales. He was electing his ministers, giving rewards to the trusted and punishments to those who were stupid enough to support the Princes.

"I haven't time to visit my dear little nephews in the Tower, Marsden," he said the day after he'd been proclaimed King. "But I do worry about them."

"They are safe in there," I assured him.

"But *are* they?" he frowned. "If any harm came to them then I would be blamed ... the way I was blamed for the death of King Henry VI. While I am in London the boys must remain alive, you understand?"

"And when you leave London?" I asked.

My lord looked at me as if he were disappointed. He repeated his words slowly. "While I am in London ...

the boys must remain alive."

"Yes, sire ... I mean, yes ... Your Grace."

"Sire will do, for my old and trusted friends." He wrapped a strong arm around my shoulder and pulled my ear close to his thin mouth. "I have a small task for you."

I thought for a moment he was going to ask me to murder the Princes. I knew that it would come some day, but I wasn't sure how I would do it ... I wasn't even sure *if* I could do it. I'd lost sleep thinking about cutting their white little throats, or hearing their cries as I placed their heads on a block. But the job he gave me was not so murderous.

An hour later I had crossed the city and arrived at the Tower.

The boys were in the garden of the royal apartments. The Constable of the Tower, Brackenbury, had set up a target and the boys were having an archery competition. I looked down on them for a while from one of the windows. One of the arrows could easily go astray, I thought. The nine-year-old Duke of York was a little clumsy. Suppose an arrow slipped and struck his older brother

Edward? Suppose it struck Edward in the heart and killed him? That would be one less problem for my master to worry about. The trouble was, the second brother would still be alive. We might get away with arranging one accident, but two accidents would look like certain murder.

One dead prince was no use. They *both* had to go. While one lived there was always a chance that someone would raise an army to help him win the throne. It was two or nothing.

I walked into the garden. The little Duke of York ran towards me with his long fair hair flowing like a golden pennant in the breeze. "Hello, Uncle Anthony!" he cried, throwing himself into my arms. I picked up his small body and swung him high into the air. (It would be such a pity if I were to drop him on his frail little eggshell skull, wouldn't it?) I put him down gently on the grass. (One was no good dead without the other, and Edward Prince of Wales was too dignified a young man to be swung round my head.)

"Hello, sire," I said, smiling.

Edward walked towards me, frowning a little. "Sire? You called me sire? Don't you usually address your king as `Your Grace'?"

He was always a fussy child, that one. His jaw was stiff and swollen. His teeth were rotting and I knew he was in pain. Since he'd been in the Tower his mouth illness had grown worse. It hurt him to eat and it hurt him to speak. I guessed that it must hurt him to smile.

"I do indeed, sire," I said. "And that is one of the things I have come to talk to you about."

We sat on a bench under the shade of a tree. It was a beautiful garden, sheltered by the high walls of the Tower from the damp draughts from the river and its foul smells. There were high white clouds in the summer sky and birds sang in the branches of the trees that were heavy with leaves. A perfect day.

Edward stood in front of me while his little brother sat on the grass at my feet. "Today, sire, all your worries are over."

"The date for my coronation has been set, then?"

"No-o. I mean you have no worries about a coronation ... because you won't be having one."

"No coronation? My robes have been made! The tailor fitted them today!"

"Mine too!" The Duke of York put in. "They're the richest blue in all the world." He looked up at the sky above him. "Bluer than the sky!"

"I'm sure you'll have the chance to wear them some day ... but for now you will not be needing them. You see, the lords of the land have had a little chat and they decided that they'd like your Uncle Dickon to be king instead."

The Duke of York's little mouth fell open and he blinked. But the Prince of Wales became wild. A true Prince of Wails! "They can't do that!" he sobbed. Tears sprang to his blue eyes and ran down his hot cheeks. He searched my face to see if it was one of my jokes. He saw no hope in my face ... but perhaps he read some of the thoughts I'd been having about an accident for him. "It's *my* throne, Marsden."

"Not any more, sire."

"I'll fight for it," he threatened.

"You'll lose, sire ... and maybe lose your life in the fighting."

"I'd rather die than ..." He stopped. He seemed to have read something in my eyes again.

"Is that what you're here for, Marsden? To murder us?" he asked.

His brother jumped to his feet. "No, Uncle Anthony, you wouldn't do that, would you?"

"I wouldn't hurt a fly," I said.

"Hurt a fly!" the older Prince spluttered. "I watched you strike Lord Stanley to the floor on the day Lord Hastings was executed."

"Ah … yes … but I did kick him under the table so he wouldn't be trampled on!"

"You nearly killed him!"

"I kept him out of trouble. He was about to come to the help of a traitor. He would have brought death on himself," I said, trying to keep the boys calm. "I was no more to blame for his cracked skull than the sword I used."

I rested my hand on my sword. The Duke of York screamed and threw himself behind his brother. (Not that it would have done him any good. If I'd wanted him, I'd have cut my way through the Prince of Wales to get him! Foolish child.)

"The King wants you alive," I said.

"I'm the King!"

"You're not!"

"I am! My father's will said I was to be the next king."

"But your father was a cheat and a liar …"

The Prince stepped forward, dragging his little brother behind him. For a moment I thought he was going to lash at me with the longbow in his hand. "You wouldn't say that if my father were alive," he shouted. "My father was six foot four inches tall and a brilliant fighter. He would kill you if he were here now."

"No, he wouldn't."

"He would!"

"He couldn't! We buried your father last week and I can't see a six-foot-four-inch corpse doing me much harm!"

Tears bubbled up in the eyes of the Prince. But he had asked for it. Fancy threatening me with his dead father. Silly boy.

"You're a swine," he sobbed. Slowly he sank to his knees on to the soft, daisy-speckled grass and cried.

Imagine if he'd become king! "The Scots are invading, Your Grace!" "Well, tell them to go away, or I'll cry and I'll cry."

His tears had no effect on me. It's not that I'm hard-hearted! Oh, no. But if you felt sorry for sheep, you'd never eat mutton stew, would you?

"Well, my princely friends," I said cheerfully, "the good news is that your Uncle Dickon is worried about your safety in the royal apartments here. He wants me to move you to the main tower. It's safer there, so dry your childish eyes."

"The rooms are like prison cells!" young York whinged.

"Yes. Very cosy," I agreed.

"There's no room for our servants."

"Servants are dangerous," I said. "Servants can be bribed to poison food! You'll have just four trusted men to guard you round the clock," I promised. "Master Slaughter and I will care for you and guard you by night."

"Are we prisoners, then?" York asked.

"I wouldn't say that," I said. (What I meant was, I wouldn't say that to your innocent little chubby face.) "Uncle Richard will be crowned king on the sixth of July and you will find out just how much he thinks of his dear little nephews!"

"So I'll get to wear my new blue robes after all?" York said excitedly.

"I don't remember seeing your name on the list of invitations," I said. "But we can have our own special celebration in your cells."

"Cells?"

"I meant rooms."

"You said 'cells'," Prince Edward said hoarsely.

"I said 'cellars' – we will raid the wine cellars for the best French wines and have a party. Now, let me show you to your ... rooms," I said. "Master Slaughter is waiting for you."

The Princes trooped after me, downhearted. "Slaughter is a strange name for the man," the young Prince said.

"Take away the 'S' and what have you got?"

"Laughter!"

"That's right. He's a bundle of laughs is Master Slaughter! He'll bring tears to your eyes!" I promised. And for once I wasn't lying to them. (I forgot to tell them his pet name was "Black Will" because his heart was as dark as a Tower raven's wing.)

Of course the coronation was a truly great occasion. Our Dickon looked like a god, not a king, in his mantle of purple cloth of gold. Master Curteys of the Royal Wardrobe said the Queen's purple dress took fifty-six yards of velvet.

The banquet after the coronation lasted nearly six hours. What I couldn't eat I stowed away in a kerchief and carried back to my little prince friends in the Tower. Master Slaughter said it was his duty to test the food for poison. But by the time he'd tested all the food there was none left for the Princes. They were asleep anyway so they

never missed it and the Prince of Wales still had no appetite. I slept the night in the guardroom of the Tower and woke with an aching gut and a burning pain behind my eyes. Perhaps one of the eight pints of wine had upset me.

The day after the coronation King Richard III (my lord Dickon) began to prepare to travel around the country so the people could meet their new king. He slapped my belly when I met him and seemed in a good mood. "Too much food, Marsden. You won't fit into your armour!"

"I'll have new armour made," I said.

The King looked at me sharply. "Let's hope you never need it."

"No, sire," I said.

"Now, Marsden, I've decided to reward loyal folk like you with some land. I thought I'd give you some rich woodland so you can do a spot of hunting when you get home. Anything in mind?"

"Bournmoor Woods, sire," I said. I wasn't greedy! They weren't huge woods but they were rich in deer and hares, and they belonged to my hated neighbour Lord Birtley. It would warm my heart to throw him out of his own woods.

"They're yours. Now, Marsden, the bad news," he said, and grinned, his small black eyes almost disappearing behind his high cheekbones. "I want you to take care of things at the Tower while I tour the country. I'd like to take you with me, but I need you here."

"I understand, sire," I said. "You want me to take care of the Princes?"

"I want you to keep them alive ..." he said, and left the words trailing like smoke on a sunset breeze.

"Until ...?"

He didn't answer directly. "I will be taking James Tyrell with me to the west country. If he arrives at the Tower with a message then you will know that it comes from me. Now get your flabby body back to the Tower, Marsden. The people want to see their king."

"I bow my flabby head to your every wish," I said, and went back.

To wait.

My Great-Uncle George stopped. My father and mother had entered the room and were waiting for our guest to join them at the breakfast table.

Humphrey Vere was looking thoughtful. He left his seat at the window and crossed the hall to bid my parents good day. Meg slipped quietly out of the room to start her serving duties.

And I thought about a grey horse. "Excuse me," I said to Vere.

"Yes, my boy?"

"Can I check your horse? See that it's had a good night

in our stable. It must be tired, after its journey."

"That's kind of you," Vere said.

I hurried round to the stable yard where Martin the Ostler was carrying a leather bucket of oats to a horse in the end stable. It was a fine dark bay colour – practically black.

"He's a beauty, Master William," Martin said. "A Spanish palfrey. Worth twice as much as our English palfreys, they say."

"And well trained," I said. "He didn't run away when his master was attacked."

The ostler slapped the beast on the neck and said, "He's worth at least ten pounds, this horse."

"And where would I go to buy a horse like this round here?" I asked, stroking the soft black muzzle.

"Wat Grey," Martin said immediately.

"And where does Wat Grey get fine horses like this from?" I asked.

Martin busied himself with the bucket and mumbled, "Best not to ask."

But I *will* ask, I thought. I will.

CHAPTER EIGHT

"A horse! A horse! My kingdom for a horse!"

At nine o'clock my father and Humphrey Vere set out for Widow Atkinson's cottage to look at the body and to recover the saddle-bag.

I met Meg at the gate that led from the kitchen garden on to the village road. "What will you say to Wat Grey?" Meg asked.

"I'll ask him if he has a grey horse for sale," I said.

"Oh, William," she said in a honey-sweet voice. "If brains were grains of gold you'd be a poor man."

"What do you mean?" I asked angrily.

"I mean," she said with her mouth turned down in disgust, "that he's not going to admit to the magistrate's son that he's got a stolen horse, is he?"

I thought about it. "Ah, but I was only going to ask him if he had a *grey* horse – not a *stolen* horse!" I reminded her.

"Oh, I forgot!" she jeered. "Wat Grey is a peasant so he *must* be stupid! That's what you people believe, isn't it?"

"Well …"

"Well, I'm sorry, William, but he's as crafty as a fox!"

I shrugged. "So long as he doesn't smell like one."

"He doesn't," she said. "He smells ten times worse."

And I thought she was joking!

She led the way down the road towards the village and

I followed nervously. There were boys in the village of my own age who used to stone me every time I rode through. I tried to talk to them, but they ran away and called me names. It seemed they hated me because of my father.

The Black Bull Tavern was the only building in the village made of brick. From the outside it looked welcoming enough in the autumn sunshine. It twisted as much as Marsden Hall although it was only half the size. There were eating and drinking rooms on the ground floor and bedrooms above. At the back there was a collection of small buildings that leaned against the wall – a place for brewing ale, a henhouse, a pigsty, a small dairy and a laundry house.

The place seemed bright and busy, but when I ducked through the low door the air was as thick as a fog on the River Wear. A suffocating smoke billowed from the coal fires smouldering in dirty chimneys and from the pipes of guests who were smoking the tobacco weed. The smells of stale ale and rotten food rose from the filthy rushes on the

floor. From some gloomy corner came the sound of a rasping snore.

"Michael the Taverner's been drinking too much of his own poison," Meg said. She squeezed between solid wooden tables which were crowded with empty ale mugs and wooden plates polished clean by the tongue of a dog that was wandering through the room, keeping one yellow eye on us.

"Michael! Wake up! Time you paid a pot boy to clear up every night, you mean, penny-pinching, close-fisted sluggard."

The snoring stopped suddenly. The flabby grey face of the landlord crumpled up into folds as whiskery as a wild boar. "Can't afford it," he said. His voice was coarse and rough, like his unshaven face.

"Michael, you're the richest man in the village," Meg said boldly. "You sell strong ale until the men are drunk, then you add water to it to make extra money. You make mutton stew from sheep that have died of old age and hide the rotten taste with herbs you find in the woods. Your bread is made from flour so coarse it wears out teeth and so expensive it should be sprinkled with golden nuggets."

Michael the Taverner rolled over and sat up on the bench where he'd been lying. "So why do people come here?" he asked.

"Because there's nowhere else for five miles, and because all the wickedness in the world is plotted here in your private little back rooms," Meg said.

"I wouldn't know about that," the man said, rising slowly and scratching his belly. "What goes on in there is private."

"What goes on in there is criminal," Meg said.

The taverner peered through the gloom and saw me for the first time. "God's nails! What's he doing here?"

"He's with me."

"He's the son of the magistrate! God's nails! He's got no right coming in here! Go on! Clear off!" he tried to shout, but broke down in a fit of coughing.

"Be polite to me, or I'll have to close this place down," I said.

Meg turned on me. "Threats like that won't work. He'll close up tighter than an oyster."

"So? What am I supposed to do?"

"Get out!"

"What? Let him throw me out of a common flea-palace like this?"

"No," she said quietly. "Let him *think* he has thrown you out of the place. I'll find out where Wat Grey is while you have a look round the horse stalls at the back for a grey horse."

"Ah! Good idea," I said.

"So do it … but make a fuss," she urged.

I cleared my throat. "You haven't heard the last of this, my man!" I said, backing towards the door.

"God's nails! Push off, you little tomfarthing!" he roared and coughed again.

"I'll see you hanging in chains!" I cried, remembering some of the acting skills I'd picked up from the travelling players.

"And I'll bite through yer chains!" he said, baring teeth that were black in the places that weren't green.

Satisfied with my performance I walked away, and then turned the corner through an arch and into a stable yard which had been swept and washed down. If Michael the

Taverner kept his taproom like a dungheap then someone kept his stable yard very clean indeed. Horses in this village were more valuable than people.

I walked from stall to stall and saw that each horse had fresh hay and water and had been brushed till its coat shone. There were two chestnut mares, a roan gelding, a piebald pony and a fine black stallion. It snickered softly as I walked past and I patted it on the neck.

The last stall was empty. I was disappointed. No grey horse. I walked back to the piebald pony and it nudged me with its nose as I walked past. I patted it on its white neck and saw that its coat had a dirty mark that spoiled the white. I put a hand on its shoulder to steady it while I looked at the neck. There was now a mark on the shoulder where my hand had rested. I pulled my hand away and looked at the palm. It was stained black!

Maybe my head was dull from the lack of sleep, but I couldn't understand how I got a black hand from stroking a white pony. Then I worked out that the black had been on my hand *before* I went past its stall. Finally it dawned on me that the only thing I'd touched was the neck of the black horse.

"That horse isn't black!" I whispered to my piebald friend. "It's been stained to look black! I'll bet you a new set of horseshoes that I can tell you what colour it is underneath!"

The piebald pony didn't take my bet so I knew I was right.

I hurried back to the front porch of the tavern where I could hear Meg talking to Michael the Taverner. He was drinking and talking freely so I just crouched down to listen. "I agree that Wat Grey is a prigger of prancers," he was saying. "But Wat wouldn't kill a man for his horse."

"He would if the man recognized him and threatened to report him to the constable," Meg argued.

"The constable doesn't bother us. A few groats in his pocket and he ignores what we want him to ignore. In fact he's probably the biggest villain in the village!"

I was shocked to think the smith had fooled my father for so many years, but didn't have time to wonder about it because Michael the Taverner was going on, "No, no! Wat Grey doesn't work like that! He's not a thief. He doesn't stop people in the woods and say, 'Your horse or your life!' No, a canter will bring horses to Wat ... a horse that may have strayed ... a horse that may have been taken from a stable fifty miles away. Wat changes their appearance and sells them for a profit. He's not a murderer! He doesn't *need* to be!"

There was the sound of ale being poured from a jug into two mugs. Then Meg asked, "So who else would wait in the woods to rob a man?"

"Aye, that's what you should be asking!" the taverner said. "It's more likely that a thief was waiting for a coney to come along and robbed him for his money! Maybe the rider died and the thief rode off on the horse."

There was a sound of drinking. Meg asked, "So did you see any thieves in here last night?"

"If I did, I wouldn't tell you!" he answered. "I make my trade by keeping secrets, not by blabbing them."

"Everyone in the village is under suspicion till the murderer is caught," Meg explained. "Sir James Marsden won't rest till he's arrested someone. He may even search this place from top to bottom."

"He wouldn't!" the taverner groaned. There was panic in his voice. "Look! Tell that Marsden brat there was no one unusual in here last night. That's the truth, Miss Meg. We had a fingerer in trying to cheat a traveller out of his money and a jackman offering forged money. We had the usual sharks and coggers trying to cheat at cards. A few clapperdudgeons going around begging. But nothing unusual."

"And no grey horse in your stable?"

"'Snails! If you find a grey horse in my stable then you can tie me to a cart tail and whip me from here to Durham!"

I rose from my crouched position and stepped into the doorway. "Take your shirt off, Michael," I said. "We may as well start the whipping now!"

He peered up at me with his red-rimmed, crusted eyes and said, "I thought I'd told you to get out."

"I got as far as your stables," I said. "I found a horse there that was quite black – except the black rubs off when you touch it."

The little red eyes blinked rapidly. "Well, I'll be a tinker's uncle! A fawney prancer in my stables, you say? God's nails! How did that get there?"

"Perhaps you can explain to my father," I said.

His bullying voice was a whine now. "Perhaps I could just explain to *you*, Master William …"

"Fine. If it's a good enough story then I may not tell him. But if you lie, then you can make that trip to Durham with a lash at your back all the way."

"You wouldn't do that," he breathed. "I'm a sick man. It's me chest. I have a bad chest."

"Probably from all the smoke in this place," I said, glad to back out into the fresh air.

He rose and shambled after me, coughing pathetically.

Meg walked alongside me and spoke out of the corner of her mouth. "You're getting better!" she said.

It was the first good thing she'd said about me. It wasn't much, but it was a start. There was a pump in the centre of the stable yard and I filled a bucket of water. I got the taverner to hold the horse's head while I slopped water down its neck. A rub with a rag showed its true colour underneath.

"Grey!" Meg said.

I turned to the innkeeper, who had turned as green as his teeth. "This is the horse of a dead man. You are helping to hide a stolen horse and maybe helping to conceal a murderer."

"Not me, master!" he moaned.

"You could hang for this."

"Oh, no!" he cried and coughed. "I couldn't climb the ladder to the scaffold. God's nails! Not with my weak chest!"

"Then we'll put you on the stolen horse with a rope around your neck, we'll tie the other end of the rope to a tree and ..."

"No! It's Wat Grey that's to blame for this!" he wailed. "I swear it! He came in yesterday evening and asked if he could hire a stable. I never asked no questions. I just told him to use this one. I wouldn't have done it if I'd known he was a murderer. 'Snails I wouldn't.'"

"I'll take this horse back to Marsden Hall," I said and took the rope from him. I led the animal back through the village and to the stables at the back of my home. Martin the Ostler took it from me.

"A fine new horse you have there, Master William," he said.

"A fine *grey* horse, Martin," I said. "Do you think you could clean it up?"

"Of course, Master William, you just leave it to me."

Meg looked satisfied as it was led away. "We've read the messages and we've found his horse. We've worked out how he was killed ... but we still don't know *why* he was killed."

"Wat Grey killed him to get the horse," I said. "We've solved the mystery!"

She frowned. "We need to see Wat Grey. Talk to him."

"Talk to a murderer? Shouldn't we leave that to Constable Smith or my father?"

"Did *they* find the horse?"

"No ..."

"And have *they* done anything to solve the mystery?"

"No ..."

"Then they needn't know anything about this until everything is finished," she said firmly.

The idea of presenting my father with a complete case was pleasant. He might have a higher opinion of me if I succeeded where he failed. "Shall we go and see Wat Grey now?" I asked.

Meg twisted her face. "I have my work to do, William. All the bedding to see to and kitchen pans to polish. I've lost enough time already this morning. The steward will be furious if I miss any more work. Can we leave it till after dinner today?"

I was worried that the horse-prigger Grey would find we'd uncovered his horse trickery and would flee from the village. Still, I collected my practice sword and began practising with the heavy oak pole that was roughly carved into the shape of a man.

I was trying my backhand swing to the neck of the figure. The joint between a man's helmet and his breastplate is weak. I could hit it five times out of ten – but in battle I knew I'd have to hit it the first time I saw an opening. "In battle there are no second chances," Great-Uncle George always said. Five times out of ten was no good – and oak poles don't fight back.

I was sweating and my arms were beginning to ache, though the practice sword is not quite as heavy as a battle sword.

"In battle there are no second chances," Great-Uncle George said. He said it as he stepped out from the doorway at the foot of the East Wing and sat on a stool to watch. The autumn sun was still warm enough for him to enjoy the sheltered yard where I did my practice ... where Marsdens had practised for hundreds of years.

I cut and struck the pole half a foot too high. "Whoa!" the old knight said. "There goes his left ear."

I blushed and was only glad Meg wasn't there watching with her cool green eyes. The next swing struck the figure even higher. "Aha! That's the way!" my great-uncle laughed. "Give the pilgarlic a haircut!"

I lowered the sword and turned to face my uncle. His face was a rich pink under the thick white whiskers – he refused to follow the fashion of shaving his face. "What's it like to kill a man, Great-Uncle?" I asked.

He leaned forward. "There are more ways to kill a man than one," he said, looking at me through his heavy white brows.

"Yes," I said. "Stab him, strangle him, poison him …"

He raised a hand. "No. I mean there are just two ways to kill a man. In hot blood and in cold blood. And each takes a different kind of man to do it. Most men can kill someone during a battle – when your blood is pounding like a drum in your head; when the men around you are screaming in rage and when you know your enemy will kill you first if he gets the chance. In the days of the old Crusades the Catholic Church forgave its soldiers for any-one they killed in battle."

"And you've killed men in battle? How many?"

"Too many."

"Could I do it, do you think?"

"You may *have* to," he said. "These sword battles against a wooden pole aren't a game, William. I fought in Henry VIII's army against the Scots, but that was a long time ago – we left our sailors to beat the Spanish Armada. We've had peace for as long as most men can remember. But if war comes, you young ones will have to be ready."

"Will war come?" I asked.

He looked up into the clear sky where crows wheeled and croaked. "I said last night that the death of a monarch makes for a dangerous time. James is a Scot and

God knows I hate the Scots – but he will bring peace. If anyone stands in his way then the Scots will attack from the north and the French will land in the south."

I thought of the letters and the danger they'd be if they fell into the wrong hands. I felt they were burning my mattress at this very moment.

"But what about cold blood, Uncle?" I asked. "Have you ever killed anyone in cold blood?"

"Ah, no. I'm not that sort of man. It takes a special kind of man to plot the death of another human being. A soldier is a soldier ... but a murderer is a devil."

"How do you know when a man is a devil?" I asked. "I mean to say ... have you ever met someone who's killed in cold blood?"

He looked up at me. "Perhaps."

"Your grandfather? Anthony Marsden? He murdered the Princes in the Tower, didn't he?"

His old face closed as if he was in pain. "Why do you want to know?"

"I want to know how to spot a murderer."

"Then I can't help you."

"But your grandfather ..."

"... always swore he had nothing to do with the deaths of the Princes in the Tower!"

Chapter Nine

"So full of fearful dreams, of ugly sights"

My great-uncle stretched his legs in front of him and rested his back against the stone wall that was warm cream in the sunlight. And he remembered ...

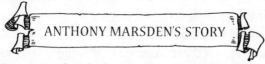

ANTHONY MARSDEN'S STORY

The Tower is a hard place to live. I think it's the ghosts. People have been executed there, people have died in the torture chambers, and people have died of cold, or poisoning, or simply of fear. But their spirits linger on, I swear it.

The young Duke of York didn't feel it. He was as happy as ever with his books and his toys and his archery practice. But the Prince of Wales seemed to take it much more to heart.

"Cheer up, Lord Edward," I said the morning after King Richard had left London. (I had to call him Lord Edward now that he wasn't even a prince.)

"I have lost everything," the boy sighed. He did a lot of sighing in those days.

"You haven't lost a thing!" I said.

He looked up with those limp blue eyes. His mother was famous for her beauty and her heavy eyelids, but Lord

Edward's eyes looked simply pathetic, like a dying rabbit's. "I've lost my crown!" he groaned.

"No, you haven't!" I said. "You never had a crown! How can you lose something you never had? Anyway, it wouldn't have fitted you. Big, heavy thing. It's back in the treasury downstairs if you want to try it on," I told him.

He shook his head. "I've lost my throne."

"What throne's that, then? I never saw you sitting on a throne! It was all in your mind! You were never crowned and you never ruled, so how can you say you've lost those things? But I'll tell you what we have lost!"

"What?"

"A whole load of treasure from downstairs. Your stepbrother was the last Deputy Constable of this Tower. They say he stole the stuff before he ran off to hide in Westminster with your mother. Imagine that! He thought you were going to be king – he ran off with the royal treasure so he was really robbing his own stepbrother! And he took it to your mother. I'll bet she was in on the robbery too! Robbing her own son. What a terrible world," I said.

"Terrible indeed, Marsden," he sighed again. (To be honest, that sighing was getting me down a bit. It would you.)

"Why, you're the luckiest young man in the world. Well away from your grasping mother and your thieving stepbrother, and Mr Slaughter and me to look after you. You should be on top of the world. Look, why not tie up the points on your doublet and come out for a spot of fresh air?"

He rolled over on his bed, turned his face to the wall and mumbled, "I can't be bothered."

What a little misery guts! Mr Slaughter and I tried everything, but he couldn't even be bothered to dress himself.

"He's not very well," his little brother told me. "His teeth hurt and he can't eat. Will he die, Marsden?"

"We'll all die, Lord York – sooner or later," I said.

As the hot July days passed in the cool gloom of the White Tower I became restless. Our Dickon wanted me here, but I wanted to get back to Marsden Manor, claim Bournmoor Woods from my neighbour and hunt and fight. The Princes weren't the only prisoners in the Tower. I felt I was a prisoner too.

So I was pleased when the Constable of the Tower, Sir Robert Brackenbury, came to us one evening when we were playing dice and Black Will Slaughter was winning a fortune from me. (I suspected he was playing with crooked dice like some trickster to trick me out of my money. I never caught him out.)

Sir Robert Brackenbury was a thin man who worried all the fat off his spindly body. Even his beard was as thin as a beggar's cloak and as colourless as a December sky. He visited the boys once a day, but it seemed to upset him –

especially when Lord Edward refused to speak or eat or rise from his bed. We'd never seen Brackenbury after dark.

He held a candle and the shadows of his eyes were huge and grey and frightened. "Sir James Tyrell is here with a message from King Richard," he said, his voice trembling.

"How is my lord Dickon?" I yawned.

"His Grace is well. But Sir James has suggested that he can take over our duties for the night."

I stopped yawning and jumped up from my stool. "A night away from here?" I cried. "Wonderful news. Dickon's a hundred miles from here, yet he hasn't forgotten us!"

"I am commanded to give up the keys of the Tower for tonight." Brackenbury shivered and quivered like a half-drowned dog.

"Come on, Will Slaughter! Let's find a tavern on the quayside and enjoy spending the money you've cheated me out of!"

Will's large jaw stuck out sulkily. "Cheated?"

"Let's just get out!" I urged him and tugged him off his stool. "A good mug of ale and a gossip with the local people. Let's hear the latest news! I feel like a man who's been released from a ten-year sentence, not ten days."

Brackenbury's face was as pale as the limewashed walls of the White Tower. I looked into his room to greet Sir James Tyrell.

"How are things in the outside world, James?" I asked.

A man stood silently at Tyrell's shoulder. "This is John Dighton," he said. "My servant."

I was hoping I'd meet livelier company in a London tavern to tell the truth, I could have found livelier company in the Tower graveyard.

"We'll be back tomorrow at daybreak!" I promised.

"Don't hurry," Sir James said. The man had always been friendly towards me, but tonight he seemed to be as cool as the mist on the Thames. "Report back to Brackenbury at sunset tomorrow. No earlier."

It meant nothing to me at the time. I was just so eager to get away from the gloomy grey walls and the cold chill of invisible spirits. I wished Sir James a good night and bowed. That's when I noticed the gilded spurs on his boots. Gilded spurs just like the ones on the masked man who'd executed Hastings.

Sir James Tyrell's servant, Dighton, did not say one word. Perhaps he'd had his tongue cut out.

Will Slaughter and I stepped on to the path along the river bank and headed towards the city.

Now I've seen every town in England and a few in Scotland and France too. But London's like no other. It's not so much a city – more a festering snake pit where every step is a danger. Every Londoner is a smiling cut-throat who wants your liver on the end of his knife and your gold in his pocket. Will Slaughter knew the best rat holes to drink in and the dark alleys to avoid.

We walked shoulder to shoulder, hands on our knives and daggers, ready to defend ourselves against the villains who would feed us as dog-meat as soon as look at us. Now I'm a brave man, but after half a mile my nerves were as tight as a lute string. I'd rather face a band of Scots cattle raiders than walk a London street after dark.

Inn signs creaked above our heads and lanterns showed the brightly painted symbols. A White Swan here and a duke's coat of arms there. Most of the windowpanes were filled with horn so we couldn't see what we were walking in to. But Black Will told me the inn with the sign of the

chessboard was cleaner than most. We found it at last at the end of London Bridge. The tower at the end of the bridge rose up into the blackness. Somewhere up there the sightless heads of traitors were stuck on poles. Even in the dark we could hear the flapping of crows stealing the hair for their nests.

The Chess Board Inn was crowded and every sort of gaming was going on inside. Cards and dice seemed to be the most popular. We found a space on a bench seat and a maid in a greasy apron came to take our order. If I ever go to Hell then I know it can't be as hot as it was that night in the Chess Board.

"A jug of ale," Will Slaughter shouted over the noise of the arguing, the cries of triumph and the groans of defeat.

The girl nodded and moved away, and I called after her. "What sort of food can you offer?" Then a strange thing happened. The noise dropped suddenly. Eyes turned towards me, as friendly as a wasp in your shirt.

A man who was only slightly wider than the door rose to his feet. The noise dropped further. His face was scarred and battered like a bear that had spent too many years being baited by dogs. "By your voice you're from the north!" he said.

My hand slipped round to my dagger. "I am."

"You're scum," he spat.

If I was going to get into a fight I wanted friends behind me and not a hundred hostile southerners. "So is your new king from the north," I said.

"That's what I'm saying," he growled. "Scum floats to the top. We don't like northerners down here."

"I know how you feel," I said. His slow brain tried to work out if that was an insult. I explained. "We have the same trouble with the Scots to the north of us."

"That villain Duke of Gloucester shut the real king and his brother away in the Tower," he went on, building up his rage.

"So I've heard."

"But there are some who think they shouldn't be in there."

"They're very comfortable," I said.

"How do you know?" he asked.

"I met a man who guards them," I said quickly.

"Well, next time you see that man tell him to start digging his grave. There are a lot of people round here who plan to put our Edward on the throne where he belongs!"

"I'll tell him," I promised.

It was so quiet in the room now I could hear Will Slaughter breathing next to me. At last the man with the torn-bear face said, "Don't forget. You tell him."

"I'll tell him."

The serving maid returned with a jug of ale and was about to place it on the table. "I like ale," the Londoner said.

"Then allow me to treat you to a drink!" I laughed. I turned to the girl. "Fill my friend's mug!"

The man said, "Don't bother." He reached across, took the jug from her and placed it to his scarred lips. He tilted his head back and in five seconds had drained it all. His friends cheered and everyone laughed at me.

"Can you do that again?" I asked.

"Can you pay?" he said.

I nudged Black Will. "We can."

My friend Will unwillingly dragged out his purse and placed a groat on the table. A second jug was delivered and followed the first almost as quickly. He had finished six before he sank back into his seat and began snoring. Then the drinkers and gamblers lost interest in us and returned to their games. It was an expensive evening, but it was better than being dead.

After several jars I felt sleepy myself. I hired a room from the landlord, climbing the twisting stairs to lie on a straw-filled mattress under a stained blanket. Will fell on the mattress next to me and was snoring as his head touched the bed.

I was not long in falling asleep beside him.

When I woke in the morning we found we were sharing the room with ten other men.

And both our purses were gone.

London is no place to spend a day without money. I was hungry and the landlord refused to give us breakfast unless I had money to pay. The only place I could go was back to the Tower.

It was mid-morning before I walked into the White Tower and met Sir James Tyrell coming out, gold spurs clattering on the granite paving. He looked startled and annoyed.

"I thought I told you not to come back till sunset."

"I need to eat and sleep," I grumbled.

"Then go to the Wakefield Tower," he snapped.

Will Slaughter and I limped tiredly round the walls to the kitchens that we'd been sent to.

After supper we felt fit enough to return to work. The winding staircases in the White Tower seemed steeper and gloomier than ever. "Well, Master York!" I called. "Have you missed us?"

The silence that met my call was deeper than the Tower dungeon. It's not just that the Princes were missing. It was more. It was as if they'd never been there. "They've been rescued!" was my first thought. I tumbled down the stairs to Constable Brackenbury's room. "The Princes!" I began.

"... have left us," he said quietly. "The King was worried about rumours of their supporters coming to take them. He's ... he asked Sir James Tyrell to ... move them to a place of safety."

And I thought that was the last I'd ever see of my little friends.

That's what I thought.

My Great-Uncle George stretched and rose to his feet. "So, you see, William, I can't help you. My grandfather always swore he had nothing to do with the disappearance of the Princes from the Tower. I can't go accusing him of being a murderer, because he isn't here to defend himself."

"But King Richard III – *he* was a murderer," I said.

"I'm sure he was, but he died long before I was born!" my great-uncle said. "No, if you are looking for a murderer, then I can't say for sure that I've ever met one."

"What's this about murder?" my father asked as he came out of the tower door with our guest, Humphrey Vere, behind him.

"Young William was wondering if you could tell a murderer just by looking at him."

"Hah," my father laughed bitterly. "I wish we could! It would make my job much easier. But at the moment I am more concerned to find a thief!"

"What's been stolen?" I asked.

"Why, some of the most secret letters ever written by Her Majesty Queen Elizabeth! Some rogue has stolen them from the saddle-bag of the dead thief over at Widow Atkinson's cottage. And if I could find out who took them I would hang him from the highest tree in County Durham!"

I felt a strange and suffocating tightness at my throat.

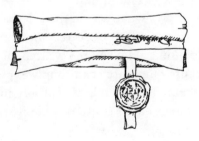

CHAPTER TEN

"His better does not breathe upon this earth"

My father began to explain the problem of the letters to my Great-Uncle George as if I wasn't there. That was his usual way of treating me, so I wasn't surprised or hurt by it.

Humphrey Vere paced the cobbled yard, restless and worried. I had thought he was so calm. Last night he'd come to us after being attacked and robbed and seemed so unruffled. Now he was agitated because his letters were missing. But he could have claimed them last night. Why wasn't he worried then? Humphrey Vere was a strange man and I didn't understand him.

"Humphrey knows what was in those letters, of course, but he is bound by an oath of secrecy not to tell us," my father was explaining. "Losing the written messages doesn't matter because Humphrey can simply explain to James what was in them. The trouble is that *any* message from the Queen to James could cause trouble if it fell into the wrong hands."

"Or the *right* hands," my great-uncle said gruffly. "Not everyone wants a Scot for a king. James is a Scot and the son of a murdering Catholic queen."

"Yes, Uncle George," my father said impatiently. "We all know how you feel about our neighbours across the border, but it's better to have peace with a Scottish king than war without one."

The old knight just blew out his cheeks and made a noise that sounded like "Pah!"

"Anyway," my father went on, "Humphrey will have to stay with us until we discover the thief and get our hands on those letters."

"It's more than the letters, Sir James," Humphrey put in. "Of course I would like to get them back, but they may not cause too much trouble. A thief would not find much to interest him in packets of paper. He may use them as tinder for a fire …"

(Or stuffing for his mattress, I thought!)

"… or he may be able to read them and sell them to Arbella Stuart's party. But we would simply say they were forgeries."

My father rubbed his hands in his fussy way he has and said, "It's good to know it is not a major scandal, losing those letters. It would not look good for the Marsden estate if it became known we had thieves wandering through our woods. People – important people – would blame the magistrate. But we will find the thief. No criminal goes unpunished in the estates of Marsden!"

I glanced at Humphrey's long handsome face. That "V"-shaped upper lip was dipping in disgust at my father's self-important claims. The cruelty was there for an instant. Even Great-Uncle George, who was used to Father's pompous ways, was blowing out his cheeks ready to explode with scorn.

Suddenly Humphrey smiled. "I am sure you will find the thief, but as I was saying, he has caused me a great problem … my passport was in that saddle-bag."

I was so close to saying, "No, it wasn't!" that I almost bit through my tongue in stopping myself.

"Her Majesty herself signed a warrant that gave me permission to travel freely through England on her business. It also gave a very strong warning to the Scots that I should be allowed a safe passage to James in Edinburgh. Then, of course, it told James that I am Humphrey Vere and I have power direct from the Queen and her ministers to talk about the succession. Without that paper I may not get safely to Edinburgh – and I'm sure I wouldn't be allowed to see James himself. After all, I could be anyone. I could be a supporter of Arbella Stuart stirring up trouble ... or I could be an assassin come to put James out of the way once and for all."

While my father rambled about the various assassination attempts that had already been made on James, I worried about the missing passport.

Humphrey Vere had been robbed by the stranger. But,

before he got clear of the woods, the stranger had been murdered and his horse had been stolen. Someone had opened the packets of letters – maybe the stranger himself, or maybe the murderer. The letters were of no interest to the killer, but the passport had gone missing. Only the murderer and I knew that. And only the murderer knew *why*.

I decided that the passport could indeed be very useful to a villain. He could travel the country, posing as the Queen's messenger, and be given the freedom of all the great houses with all their great riches.

Yes, the letters were trouble – but that passport was a doorway to riches. When my father paused for breath I cut in. "Could anyone use the passport?" I asked.

My father spluttered and looked furiously at me, but Humphrey turned and said, "That's a good question!"

My father's face twisted into a pained smile. "A very good question. I was just going to ask it myself!"

Great-Uncle George snorted softly and hid a smile in his thick white beard.

"It would be difficult," Humphrey explained. "The passport describes me – five foot ten inches, dark-brown hair and no beard, grey eyes and aged twenty-seven years. Then I have signed the paper with my name; the Queen's Secretary Sir Robert Cecil has witnessed it."

"So, someone who looks like you and who can copy your signature could use the passport?" I asked.

"Precisely my question," my father put in.

Humphrey Vere shrugged. "I suppose so."

"The problem is," my father went on as he moved to stand between me and our visitor, "the problem is what are we going to do about Humphrey's passport?"

"I thought the problem was to find the thief?" Great-Uncle George said, with a wicked twinkle in his faded eyes.

"Well ... that *too*. Yes! I have a plan to discover and arrest the thief," my father said. "But first, the passport. What I suggest is that *I*, Sir James Marsden, Magistrate of the Marsden Manor in north-east Durham, should sign you a passport. Oh, yes, I know it is not so great as the passport you lost from Sir Robert Cecil, the Queen's Parrot ... as she calls him. But my name is known throughout the north and into Scotland itself. If you ride north under my protection then you ride as safely as if you had a guard of a thousand men! Oh, yes, the name James Marsden brings terror to the hearts of every evil-doer from York to Edinburgh!"

It was quite a speech. Great-Uncle George couldn't close his mouth firmly enough to make a "Pah!" In fact he looked uncertain whether to laugh or explode.

But Humphrey Vere wasn't laughing. His voice was suddenly low and respectful. "Oh, Sir James. If ... if you could do that, then Her Majesty would be in your debt."

"And, just as important, our next king would come to know and respect the name of Marsden," my father said.

"Of course!" Humphrey said smoothly. "Such a passport could save England from a terrible war. Your name would be written in letters of gold in the history of this country."

"Alongside Sir Francis Drake, Sir Walter Raleigh and Sir Martin Frobisher!" my father whispered.

"Yes, they were all fools and dreamers," Great-Uncle George muttered.

"I'll arrange for a secretary to draw up a passport now –

and it will have my wax seal upon it, of course."

"Of course." Humphrey nodded, and the two men headed towards the house.

"The thief!" Great-Uncle George cried.

"Where?" my startled father said.

"You said you had a plan to find the thief. If you *do* find him then there would be no need to draw up a new passport," the old man explained patiently.

The agony of losing his place in the history books seemed to pass across my father's face. "Ah, yes," he said dully. "The thief. My idea was to contact all the local horse thieves and demand that they tell us all they know about the missing horse."

My mouth went dry. If Father went to the village tavern, then the odious Michael would tell him that I had taken the horse. "Father …" I began.

"Silence, boy, don't interrupt," he snapped. "No, I believe the answer to the mystery lies with the disappearance of the horse. Sadly, Humphrey here didn't see the dead man ride away so we don't know what colour the horse was. And a tired horse would not have wandered far. It must be in the hands of the local priggers. I will question that Wat Grey first," my father said. He turned to Humphrey Vere. "I know all the criminals in this region. Show me a crime and I can tell you who has done it in two minutes. I'm never wrong. Hardly need to bring them to the magistrate's court, you know."

"Really?"

"Oh, yes, indeed. I am the terror of the local criminal brotherhood. They fear me more than they fear the Devil himself. Oh, yes! I will question Wat Grey and arrest him. This time he may even hang for murder and that will be good riddance to another kinchin-cove. The horses for a hundred miles around will sleep happier in their stables knowing he is swinging from a tree by his miserable neck."

"How will the horses know?" Great-Uncle George asked.

Father flashed him a look of irritation and walked towards the door. As he disappeared Martin the Ostler came from the stable yard leading a shining grey horse. "Here he is, Master William – shiny as Sir George's nose ... ooh! Sorry, Sir George ... didn't see you sitting there."

"Next time I come to the stables you'd better be sure there are no horsewhips lying around, or I'll give you a taste of one!" he growled.

"That'll be nice," Martin grinned. "I've never tasted a horsewhip before. Is it better than the food that cook serves us for dinner?"

Before the old knight could rise and box his ears, Humphrey Vere walked across to the horse and stroked its muzzle. "A fine creature," he said. "You're lucky to own such a horse."

With my great-uncle and the ostler standing there I couldn't lie and pretend it was mine. "I ... I think it's the horse that belonged to the murdered man. It was in the stables behind the village tavern."

Humphrey looked at me sharply. "Shouldn't you tell your father?" he asked.

"I suppose so," I mumbled.

"The saddle-bag was with the corpse – but where is its saddle?" he asked.

"I don't know. I expect Wat Grey has it ... if he hasn't sold it already."

"You think Wat Grey killed to get this horse?"

"No. I think someone else killed the stranger to rob him the horse went free and Wat Grey prigged it for himself."

"I see. The saddle may have given us some clue as to who the man was. Never mind. Perhaps your father will squeeze a confession out of Grey," Humphrey said.

"Hah! Your father couldn't squeeze a pip out of an orange," Great-Uncle George chortled.

Martin the Ostler asked, "What should I do with the horse?"

"Keep it till my father comes home. I'll tell him about it then."

The man nodded and began to lead the horse away. "Your own horse is ready when you need him, sir," he said to Humphrey Vere. "He's groomed and fed and ready to go. Your saddle-bags are in the tack room. Shall I bring them to the Manor House for you?"

"No!" Humphrey said quickly. "I'll collect them for myself."

"I thought your saddle-bag was stolen," I said.

"Just the one with the letters inside," he said.

"But how did the thief know?" I asked.

"He probably unstrapped it and had a quick look in while I was unconscious on the ground. If he wanted to travel light he'd only take what he went after – the letters."

"I see," I said. I wandered back to the practice pole to try that backhand cut to the neck again.

After watching for a few minutes Humphrey walked over and said, "Fight me."

"What?"

"For practice," he said. "I may be able to show you a few tricks that will come in useful in battle."

Great-Uncle George leaned forward on his stool and said, "Go ahead, William. There are blunt practice swords and boiled leather armour in that chest inside the door."

So I spent the morning fighting for my life. No matter what sword stroke I tried Humphrey Vere had a counter stroke. When I blocked his sword blows then his dagger was thrust at my kidneys or my neck. After over an hour I got a blow to his head followed by a chopping to his leg, and he fell backwards. Great-Uncle George cheered and Humphrey Vere laughed. "Well done, Master William. You learn quickly."

I learned that there are no rules in a real fight. Humphrey Vere, with sharpened weapons in a real fight, would be deadly. Great-Uncle George ordered a servant to bring us ale while we sat on the cobbles and rested.

"You are a good street-fighter, Master Vere," the old man said. "Have you ever been in a full-scale battle, though?"

"No," our guest admitted. "Is it any different?"

"Ah, yes. As different as your fighting with practice swords and fighting with sharp steel to the death. You see, you don't have to worry about fighting one man, you have to worry about fighting one after another. If you knock a man down, then there's another there to take his place."

"But you have your own friends to help you, Great-Uncle," I said.

He leaned forward and said, "They're the ones you have to worry about most of all! If they turn and run away then you're alone and shaking hands with your last friend Death."

"Which battles have you fought in, sir?" Humphrey asked.

I'd heard the stories a dozen times and would gladly have heard them again. But Great-Uncle George wasn't in the mood to tell of his own glories. He said simply, "I fought at Solway Moss in 1542 – when the Scots took one look at us and ran away."

"You were so terrifying?" Humphrey smiled.

"It wasn't that. Their king decided not to go to the battle himself and he didn't even bother to send a commander to take his place. The lords couldn't agree who was in charge so no one ended up in charge! Battles are different from the fighting you do. Men need to be *organized* and *led* in a battle. The Scots had no one to urge them forward, so they got within forty paces of us and turned and walked away. We shot a few in the back and drove a few more into the marshes where they drowned. It was hardly worth the name 'battle'."

"But you fought at Pinkie," I reminded him.

"Aye, that was in 1547. We met the Scots in a real and

bloody battle outside Edinburgh. But it was nothing compared to the battles of a hundred years ago. At Pinkie our guns and cannon cut men down like a sickle cuts corn. But a hundred years ago men fought hand to hand and face to face with their enemy. That took courage. That took leadership. And kings really did go on to the battlefield and fight to the death. And battles really did change the path of history. We've got the last Tudor queen on the throne now – but the first Tudor only won the crown by fighting and killing for it."

"At Bosworth Field?" Humphrey asked.

"Aye. Bosworth Field. The last great battle. My grandfather was there, you know. Anthony Marsden fought alongside his lord, King Richard III."

"The murderer," our guest said.

"Some say that," Uncle George said. "But call him murderer, villain, traitor or thief, you could never accuse him of being a *coward*! I was telling William here the story earlier ..." he said, and went on with his grandfather's tale.

CHAPTER ELEVEN

"And make poor England weep in streams of blood"

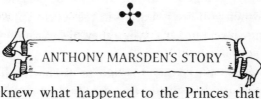

ANTHONY MARSDEN'S STORY

I never knew what happened to the Princes that night, though many have accused me of doing them to death. The Constable of the Tower, Brackenbury, said they'd been taken away to safety and that was the truth as far as I knew it. Of course there was no need for me to stay in the Tower with no one left to guard, so I came home to Marsden Manor.

The first thing I did was call on my neighbour Lord Birtley. His family had owned lands in the north since the days of the Vikings and he believed he was better than a small estate owner like me. "Sell me Bournmoor Woods," I said.

"There is a pile of horse dung six foot high at the back of my stables. I'd rather take a wooden spoon and eat every scrap of that horse dung than sell the woods to you. I've got the finest, tastiest deer in England living in those woods. Fit for a lord ... but not fit for some bully boy like you, Marsden," he sneered.

"I'll give you a thousand marks," I said.

"Your travels to London have left you deaf, Marsden. I will not sell Bournmoor Woods to you at any price."

"In that case I will take them," I said, and showed him Richard's warrant granting them to me. His bloated red face turned purple. He struggled to find words. I saved him the trouble. "If I ever catch you in Bournmoor Woods again, Birtley, I'll string you up for crow food." Then I walked out.

Now, let this be a warning to you. Be careful who you upset when you are going up in the world ... it's for sure that they'll remember it when they meet you on your way down in the world!

Of course I tied my fortune to Richard's horse tail. While he was king I was fine. But he had problems from the start. That Buckingham was given control of Wales, but he wanted more. I never trusted the man. And those southerners never really took my lord Dickon to their miserable, shrivelled, walnut hearts.

But my lord Dickon didn't need me to defeat Buckingham. God did that. Ten days of rain flooded the rivers and drowned families in their beds. Babies were floating over their fields in cradles and sheep died on the hills. Buckingham's army was washed away that winter and the man was executed in the marketplace in Salisbury. "Let me meet you and talk to you, Richard!" he wrote.

Richard never replied.

Then, some time in 1484 God turned against us. Richard's only son, Edward, died ... he was always a sickly child. Then on 16 March 1485 Richard's wife Anne died.

For the funeral I travelled down to London and met a different man to the one I'd left two years before. His thin face was pinched and pale and miserable. His eyes were haunted. "The dreams, Marsden," he said to me on the night before the funeral. "The dreams that come at night.

It gets so that I daren't lay down my head to sleep."

As they lowered his dead queen's coffin into the grave he wept.

He asked me to stay in London a while longer. He wanted people around him he could trust. I couldn't refuse.

Now it's often said, and I've noticed it's true, that troubles come in threes. Two deaths had squeezed Richard dry of his tears. I thought the news that came that summer – the third trouble – would have crushed him.

A distant cousin, Henry Tudor, was massing an army in France to invade England and take Richard's throne.

"Bad news, sire," I said.

"It's wonderful news, Marsden!" he cried, his eyes afire with joy.

"It's ... wonderful news, sire. Of course it is. We'll be invaded, we'll fight and be beaten. We'll be killed if we're lucky. If we're not lucky we'll be captured and tortured. Exactly which bit of that lot is the good news, sire?"

He faced me and placed a hand on each shoulder. Those sword-grip hands were as strong as ever. "Action,

Marsden! Action! The chance to fight for a crown, Marsden! What more can a man ask?"

"I don't have a crown," I reminded him.

"You have your precious Bournmoor Woods, don't you?" he asked.

"That's true."

"Well, if we lose the battle with Henry Tudor you will certainly lose your precious woods!"

"That's if I don't lose my even more precious life."

"Marsden," he said. "I need men from the north for this battle. Men like you and your loyal fighters. Send for them."

When a king orders, then you obey. But it was hard to feel the same joy for the coming battle that Dickon felt. Maybe it was the strange signs in the heavens. Not just the rains that washed Buckingham's army away; on the day the Queen was buried, the sun had turned black in the sky. Clever men said it was something called an eclipse. To stupid men like me it was a sign of some terrible doom.

The army led by Henry Tudor landed on 7 August over in the western corner of Wales – just two years since I'd last seen the Princes in the Tower. But I was more worried about collecting my men and arming them and training them. In two years they'd forgotten some of the drill that had made us a fearsome force.

We headed for Atherstone near Leicester and the King called his captains into his tent to explain his plans. "Lord Stanley has sent a message saying he is too ill to lead his men."

"Must have been the crack on the head that Marsden gave him!" a captain joked.

Two years ago Dickon would have laughed too, but his

grim face was white as a crow-picked skull. He waited for the laughter to die and went on, "I have reports that Stanley has two thousand men at Atherstone. If he recovers in time then he will be a great help."

Some captains and lords mumbled about treason and wanted to attack Stanley without waiting for Henry Tudor. "I'll tell you what Stanley wants," Richard said. "He wants to see which way the battle will go ... then he'll join in on the winning side."

"I wish I could do that," I grumbled. Richard's mood had caught the captains and killed their humour. Someone suggested that removing my head from my shoulders would close my treacherous mouth. Richard explained it was my idea of a joke.

But he was a great leader. He'd studied the land and told us we would line up on Ambien Hill. "If Henry Tudor wants my crown then I'll be wearing it. If Henry Tudor cares to take it then he'll have to fight his way to me and win it ... and he'll be fighting uphill. And I will kill him!"

We all cheered. There was a sort of excitement among the men and the captains that I can't explain. War is a terrible and a bloody business. And fear is a thrill and the thought of death sets your heart racing like a broken-winged bird when you pick it up.

But the screams from Richard's tent in the darkness chilled us. "It's the dreams," said our commander, the Duke of Northumberland. "He's having the dreams again."

Perhaps we slept an hour or two the night before the battle. Richard was stirring before anyone. He was a thin figure on a huge white horse, and his face was as pale as the horse. "Witches ride white horses," one of the Marsden estate men whispered.

"Who says?" I asked angrily.

"My mother told me!" he said.

"Then your mother is as stupid as her son. If Henry Tudor splits your skull then he'll feast on the porridge that runs out."

The men laughed and went quietly about preparing for the battle as the sun rose amber-gold over the rich green English fields. The last sunrise that some of them would see and the fields that would make gory graves for them. I put those cheerful thoughts at the back of my mind and checked with my group of a hundred men that they knew their places in the battle. "At the back!" someone joked.

In fact it was truer than he knew. The Duke of Norfolk's men were at the front, the King's men behind and Northumberland's men at the back.

Suddenly Richard appeared on his white horse leading a young man riding a bay pony. The young man had lank hair and a hangdog face. The war horse shouldered my men out of its way as Richard headed straight for me. "Marsden!" he shouted.

Now he was in the polished steel of his full armour. His face looked out through the raised visor and his dark eyes shone brighter than the glimmering steel.

"Sire?"

"There's a special task for you."

"In your bodyguard?" I cried excitedly.

"No, here at the rear. This young man is a hostage. His father is Lord Stanley." The young man glared at the king.

I looked to the south. Lord Stanley's men were waiting to attack … but it seemed they hadn't decided who they were going to attack! Richard raised an arm and pointed across the valley. "Watch Stanley! If he turns his army against us, then you will kill this miserable puppy that he calls a son. Kill him slowly and painfully."

"And if he fights on our side?"

Richard's thin lips gave a tight smile. "Then set this fine young man free to enjoy life as a hero of an English victory."

"Yes, sire," I said.

For a few moments Richard looked at me. "I trust you, Marsden."

They were the last words my lord Dickon ever said to me. He wheeled his war horse back to the front of the army, raised his sword and ordered the Duke of Norfolk to lead the charge. From the hill top the charge was a powerful one, but the Welsh foot soldiers with their pikes stood firm, and hacked and hewed at our knights under the streaming banners of red dragons.

Richard waited and watched as the Duke of Norfolk's men threw themselves at the spiked hedge of steel and killed and bled and died. The dust of the battle rose and rolled up the hill as the midsummer sun rose higher in the sky. Young Stanley turned to me. "May I have some water?" he asked.

"Ask your father when he gets here," I told him. I took his arm and dragged him closer to the crest of the hill so we'd have a better view of the battle in the valley below.

"My father won't be fighting for Richard," he said above the clash of metal, the thunder of hooves and the screams of the dying.

"You'll die!" I said.

He nodded. "My father says he has other sons."

I had killed men in battle and I'd even helped in the execution of the traitor Hastings. But the thought of killing a young man in cold blood was making me sick to the stomach. "I trust you, Marsden," Richard had said. "I trust you."

I turned away from young Stanley and watched the Duke of Norfolk turn his horse for a fresh charge at the foot soldiers. Somewhere in the swirl of dust he vanished from the horse and fell under a flailing storm of cold steel.

To my left the King watched his commander die and then looked over the heads of the struggling men. He leaned forward in the saddle and cried, "Henry Tudor! There he is under that red banner! I want my mounted knights with me!"

There was a scramble for the knights to collect their chargers. About eighty of them gathered round Richard, drew their battle axes, swords, lances and maces and formed a line along the ridge.

The foot soldiers had left a gap to their left and gave Richard a clear gap through to where Henry Tudor stood with his bodyguard around him. The King spurred his white horse forward and swept down the hill in a charge of streaming colours and glinting weapons.

"It's suicide!" young Stanley gasped.

"It is ... but it's a glorious way to die," I said.

Below I could make out the gold crown of the King leading the thundering horses till they clashed with a boom that sounded like someone knocking on the gates of Hell itself.

First Henry's standard-bearer was swept from his horse by Richard's vicious strokes. Then a huge knight who waited in front of Henry Tudor was smashed out of his saddle.

"He might just do it. It's impossible ... but he might just do it!" I said to the young man. But my prisoner was

looking to his left. His father's army was moving, and moving quickly. The fastest horses reached the heart of the battle and there was no doubt now whose side they were on. As my Dickon reached within a few strides of Henry Tudor his force was swept aside by the rush of Lord Stanley's knights.

But there was nowhere to go. To Richard's right there was a swamp. His horse sank, struggling. Foot soldiers with long hooked pikes rushed forward and dragged my king from his saddle.

I lost sight of him under the blood-hungry mass of Welshmen. The swampy waters at the foot of Ambien Hill were stained red. They say he died calling for a fresh horse. They say his poor, twisted body was stripped and carried off on a horse to be shown in public to the people of Leicester. They say his crown was found and handed to the greatest traitor of all, Lord Stanley. And it was Lord Stanley who placed my Richard's crown on Henry Tudor's head.

I wouldn't know. I saw none of that. My eyes were filled with tears for the first time since I was a baby. Perhaps it was the battle dust making them water.

My prisoner turned to me. "So you must do your duty," he said.

"No," I told him.

"Richard said he trusted you."

"I know what he said."

"So why don't you kill me?"

"What would be the point?"

"Revenge?"

"And then what? Your father would find out that I had killed you and then take his revenge on me. But if I let you live … I may escape with my life. I may see Marsden Manor again."

"He trusted you, Marsden."

"I know. Everyone betrays you in the end. You can't trust anyone."

The young man gave me a look of disgust.

He wasn't half so disgusted with me as I was with myself.

CHAPTER TWELVE

"I am determined to prove a villain"

Great-Uncle George stared into his cold pipe bowl as if he was wondering whether or not to light it. He pointed the stem at me. "When I was a lad I learned all about science. I never told you that, did I?"

"No, Great-Uncle."

"I learned that the universe is made up of just four elements. Earth and water, fire and air. Everything is a mixture of these four elements."

I nodded. I knew this from my own lessons.

"And humans are made up of the same four elements, but we are all mixed just a little differently," Great-Uncle George said. "A man with too much water is a cold character and a man with too much air is a dreamer. But the man with too much fire is hot-tempered. And when we get into a fight we all catch fire and do things we'd never do when we are calm. Isn't that true, Master Vere?"

"I've felt that myself," Humphrey admitted.

"So who is the most dangerous man?" my great-uncle asked me suddenly.

"The one with too much fire the hot-tempered one, of course!" I said.

The old knight shook his head slowly. "No the man with too much water in his make-up is the most dangerous. The man with the coldest blood. He plans calmly and gets what he wants quite ruthlessly. His very soul is cold. I am always amazed at the story of Richard III's death. Richard had killed King Henry VI, killed his own brother Clarence, had his old friend Hastings executed on the spot and even planned to murder his helpless little nephews. *That's* a cold-blooded man. But the man who died on Bosworth Field fought with all the heat of a furnace."

"So which one was he?" Humphrey asked. "Was he a cold-blooded killer of kings, or a hot-blooded battler?"

Great-Uncle George raised his heavy white eyebrows. "Who knows? Perhaps the hot-blooded fighter at Bosworth was the real Richard."

"And the murders?" our guest asked.

"Perhaps he never committed them," my great-uncle said.

"But the Princes died," said the stranger.

Somewhere under the thick white beard my great-uncle gave a small smile. "Did they?"

Neither Humphrey nor I had an answer to that strange question. My great-uncle went on, "After dinner it is a Marsden custom to tell stories, as you saw last night. Tonight, Master Vere, I will tell you all a curious tale about a prince. A prince of rags and patches. A prince of air and dreams."

"Tell us now, Great-Uncle," I urged.

"No. We must use the hours of daylight to find who killed that stranger in the wood."

"My father is looking into it," I said.

"Ah, but would your father recognize a cold-blooded killer if he met him?" he demanded. "The cold-blooded man is so cunning he can disguise himself as a normal man and deceive you! Is your father clever enough to see through the disguise?"

"Yes!" I said.

Great-Uncle George raised just one amused eyebrow. "When the elements were mixed in your father he had too much earth in his mixture. He is solid and slow and has no imagination. He believes what he sees."

"Don't we all?" I laughed.

"You saw a black horse at the village inn. Did you believe it?" he asked.

"Well ... not when I saw the black stuff on my hand," I said.

"Exactly. If we are going to discover the killer we need to see the grey horses under the black ones! We need to see the prince under the rags and patches – or the beggar under the velvet gown." He rose to his feet and said, "I'm off to talk to Widow Atkinson."

"Do you know her?" I asked.

He chuckled. "I've lived here all my life. Jane Atkinson and I were children together. She was Jane Fell then. She's the wisest person I've ever met."

Humphrey Vere watched as the old man walked slowly out of sight. "An interesting man," he said. "Very clever."

"Very," I agreed.

"More sword practice, Master William?" he asked.

"No ... I need to see a man in the village. Perhaps tomorrow ... if you're still here," I offered.

"I may be. If your father gets me the passport then there's nothing to stop me from leaving. I'd just like to stay a little longer to see if the Queen's letters turn up."

I turned away from him to hide my blushes and ran round to the kitchen. Meg was standing at the kitchen

table kneading dough to make the bread for the evening meal. Flour covered her face where she had wiped off sweat. "Can we go and talk to Wat Grey now?" I asked her.

"Shall I bring the dough with me?" she asked, wide-eyed.

"No ..."

"Then who do you imagine is going to finish making the bread?"

"Well ..."

"Or perhaps your lordships and ladyships can have dinner tonight without any bread?"

"We couldn't do that."

"Then get your fine jacket off, roll up your fine linen sleeves and help me," she said.

I obeyed. I don't know why! It just seemed so sensible. Kneading bread is harder work than it looks and I was soon sweating too. It took almost a quarter of an hour till we had finished to Meg's satisfaction. She took my dough, gave it a further kneading to neaten up the stringy mess I'd made, then divided the mess into loaves and placed them in the oven. She wiped her hands and face with a damp rag and passed it to me to do the same.

"I haven't much time," she said. "I have work to do.

If it's not done now, then I'll have to work into the night to get it finished, you know."

"But finding a killer is more important," I said.

"Try telling that to the steward," she said, and walked down the path with her bouncing stride.

Michael the Taverner was sitting in the midday sun, enjoying a flagon of his own wine. "Can you tell us where we'll find Wat Grey?" I asked.

"Find him yourself," he spat.

Meg jumped forward and snatched the flagon from the ground at his feet.

"Here! That's best sack!" he cried, struggling to his feet.

"It would be a shame to see it spilled then," she said, and tipped the neck down till the golden wine began to drip out.

"I'll flay you alive!" he threatened. He picked up a knife he'd been using to pare a piece of cheese.

"No, you won't," she said.

"I will!"

"Master William here would defend me. He has his sword," she said. I couldn't say it was my blunt practice sword in case he decided to attack us.

"I'm not scared of him!" he roared. He bared his green teeth menacingly.

"Fine," Meg said, letting another splash fall on the ground. "But you couldn't catch me anyway!"

The man scowled and his red eyes turned to me. "No ... but I could catch your master and skin him alive instead."

"That wouldn't get your wine back," she said.

"It would be worth a flagon of wine just to slip a knife under his lily-white skin," he purred, his red eyes as vicious and small as a wild boar's.

"His father's a magistrate," Meg warned.

"And Master William is a wine-thief, so I can do what I like to him."

"His father would have you whipped in the stocks," Meg taunted. She spilled another drop on to the road.

"There's no room in the stocks," Michael sneered. "Wat Grey's already there!"

Meg blinked. "Why, thank you, Michael! That's what we wanted to know!" She threw the wine flask at the taverner and laughed as he juggled with it to try to save his precious Spanish wine.

Meg ran to the village green which was quiet now at midday. Most people were working in the fields or indoors eating.

We found Wat Grey, a lonely and miserable figure in the stocks. At first I thought his foul-smelling feet were covered by grey stockings, but then I realized they were bare. The feet were simply filthy.

He looked up wearily. The deep lines in his pinched, foxy face were etched with dirt. Sweat trickled down and left clean lines, though a bitter wind blew his grey-streaked hair off his face. "Good morning, Master Marsden," he said cheerfully. "How's your dear father the magistrate?"

"He's well, Mr Grey."

The man sighed. "Pity. I was hoping he might have died, or be suffering from some slower and more painful death. Leprosy would be nice."

I glared at the insolent man. "My father didn't put you in these stocks," I said. "You put yourself here with your lawless behaviour!"

I felt Meg tugging at my cloak and leaned back to hear her

whisper in my ear. "Be careful what you say," she muttered.

"Why?" I asked her.

"Because you sound a complete curpin. Just like your father. Wat Grey'll just laugh at you," she explained.

There was no need for her to be so crude, I thought, but he certainly didn't look too worried. "What would *you* do?" I challenged her.

"Threaten him!" she said.

"With what?"

"Torture."

"What!"

"I'll show you," she smiled and sat next to the villain. His eyes flicked towards her nervously. "Come to set me free, Miss Meg?" he asked.

"No," she said gently. "Just come to ask you a few questions."

He opened his eyes wide. "But I don't know anything," he said. "I told Magistrate Marsden I didn't know anything, and that's why he shut me in the stocks. Doesn't bother me!"

Meg smiled. "We'll see. Now, Wat, there was a grey horse in the stable at the back of the tavern ..."

"Now what a strange place to put a horse!" he laughed.

Meg looked at him, unsmiling. "We think the horse may have belonged to a dead man."

"That's strange. How did he ride it if he was dead?" Grey asked. I had to hide a smile.

Meg stayed calm. "The man was found in a ditch on the Durham road," she said patiently. "His horse was found at the inn. We know that you put the horse there."

The horse thief's innocent face closed suddenly. "Who said that?"

Meg ignored him. "Now you can tell us how you came

across the horse and when you found it …"

"Or what?" the man sneered. He spat at the girl, but she dodged out of the way of the spittle and walked towards me.

"Henry VIII had a great idea," she said. "He had the hands cut off thieves so they couldn't ever do it again."

The man's good humour seemed to have faded. He grasped a wrist with each hand and clutched them to his thin chest. "You can't do that," he said, but he didn't sound too sure.

"I think the best way to stop a horse thief would be to cut off his feet," she said.

The feet twitched in the stocks and the twisted toes seemed to curl up.

"Give me your knife, William," she said to me.

"But …" I began to explain.

"Don't worry. If you're not prepared to cut off his feet, then I will," she said.

She took the knife from my hand and walked towards the man in the stocks. "I'll be crippled!" he moaned.

"It won't bother you," she shrugged. "You won't miss your feet because you'll bleed to death first."

"You wouldn't really do it!" he shouted.

"Are you sure?" she asked. "You have a nasty habit of laming horses by cutting the tendon in the heel, don't you? Maybe I'll just do that to you."

She waved my knife under his nose. At first he drew his head back sharply. Then he relaxed and looked her in the eye. "You'll need a sharp knife to do that, Miss Meg," he said. His voice had dropped back to its regular whine.

"And what's this?" she asked.

"It's a blunt knife," he said.

"What?" she asked, testing the edge.

"It's my practice knife," I said. "I practise with a knife and sword that have no edge to them. I tried to tell you!"

Wat Grey was laughing till he shook. The girl's face turned as red as a haw berry and she threw the knife to the ground. She turned and ran round the back of a near-by house. The man in the stocks looked at me. "Funny things, women," he sighed.

"What do you know about the horse?" I said sternly. I'd watched my father make villagers tremble when he used that tone of voice and that expression. It didn't seem to be working for me.

"Nothing," the man said.

I heard a deep bleating sound behind me and looked around to see a grim Meg leading a goat by its tether on to the green. She handed the rope to me without a word. While I held it she ran back into the house and returned with a leather bucket. She threw some white liquid over his feet. "Ooosh!" he gasped. "A bit cold that, Miss Meg!"

The liquid washed the dirt off his feet and dripped greasy grey on to the grass.

"It's water with salt in," Meg explained. "Now, Wat, you're an expert with animals. What do goats like more than anything?"

His mean little eyes flickered like a drunken butterfly. "Salt," he said.

"Salt," Meg said. She took the rope from me and led the goat towards the man. It sniffed and strained to reach the salt water on the man's feet.

"Goats don't eat feet," he said. His voice was hoarse.

"No," she agreed, and gave the goat a little more tether. The animal stretched forward and began to lick the soles of Wat Grey's feet with its rough tongue.

"Ahhhh!" he sighed, and his whole body shook. Then the sigh turned to a scream of agony and he was bouncing on the seat of the stocks till it seemed it might break. "Get it off!"

"Will you talk?" Meg asked calmly.

"I'll talk … I'll-talk-I'll-talk-I'll-talk!" he sobbed.

Meg pulled the goat back and handed it to me. "Did you know this is an old French torture?"

I looked at Wat. He was trembling. I simply shook my head.

"Now, Wat, you found a grey horse walking along the path at the edge of Bournmoor Woods?"

"Yes," he mumbled sullenly.

"You took it to the village tavern, sold the saddle and coloured the horse black."

"Yes."

"But you didn't kill the man to get it?"

"What do you take me for?" he snarled.

Megan answered by pouring salt water over his feet. "Just answer the questions, Wat."

"No … I didn't."

◆ 136 ◆

"Do you know who did?"

"No ... I followed the horse's trail back to the herb patch. Widow Atkinson was there. We followed a trail through the herbs and found the body under a pile of branches. I didn't want to get mixed up in it, so I told the old witch to report it."

"Did you see the saddle-bag beside the body?"

"I may have done."

Meg let the goat have a little more tether and its nose brush the man's foot. He jumped and Meg said, "Just say yes or no, Wat."

"Yes."

"And did you open it?"

"I might have ... ah! Yes!"

"And what did you find there?"

"Letters."

"And were they sealed?"

"No! I mean ... yes. They had seals on them, but the seals had been broken."

I stepped forward. "Was there a passport letter in with the paper packets?"

"How would I know?" he sneered. "I couldn't read the things! All I know is they were no use to me and there was no use risking a hanging for stealing them, so I put them back."

"And did you see anyone near the body?" Meg asked.

He hesitated and she let the goat move forward. "I'm thinking! I'm thinking! I'm thinking!" he cried. "I'm trying to help you! If I saw someone there then you would-n't suspect me of murder ... but I didn't."

Meg turned to me. "The killer had time to drag the body into hiding and read the letters. He'd have been gone by the time Wat found the body."

"I suppose so."

"What were you doing in the woods?"

"Nothing … no! Keep that goat off me feet! I was just snaring a few rabbits for Michael in the tavern!"

"So did you see anyone else on the Durham road?"

"Just a man on a bay horse. But he was cantering too fast for me to see much of him."

"Before or after you found the body?"

"Five minutes before," he said.

"A stranger?"

"A stranger."

Meg looked at me. She raised her eyebrows under her tangle of hair. "I've nothing else to ask," she said.

She led the goat off the green and returned it to its owner before joining me on the path back to Marsden Hall.

"That was cruel," I said.

Her small face creased with a hard scowl. "It was a dreadful, brutal thing to do," she admitted. "Making that poor goat lick those disgusting feet. So very cruel to the goat, I agree!"

"I meant it was cruel to the man!"

She looked at me with wide eyes. "But it was *fun*!" she laughed before she ran off back to the kitchens.

Chapter Thirteen

"The king's name is a tower of strength"

✤

The afternoon brought clouds and a chill wind off the river. It was growing dark before supper now and we were glad to draw the table just a little closer to the fire in the great hearth. The Marsden coat of arms was carved in stone above the mantel – a dragon being struck through the eye by a knight's lance. Underneath is the family motto.

"What does it say?" Meg asked.

"*Nemo me impune*," I told her.

"That's clever," she said sourly. "I don't read and I don't understand French either. What does it *mean*?"

"It's not French, it's Latin," I corrected her, just to irritate her a little more. "It means, 'No one harms me and escapes, or Great-Uncle George says it means, 'If you lay one finger on me, I'll tear your head off!'"

Meg giggled and went on preparing the table as the family gathered for the evening meal of venison pasties. My father came in with Humphrey Vere, explaining, "Wat Grey finally cracked after a day in the stocks."

"So what did he tell you about the theft of the horse and the robbery?"

"He says he knows nothing," my father smiled. "That

means we can forget about him and look elsewhere for the villain."

"You believe the man?" Humphrey asked as he bowed to my mother and took his seat next to her.

"Wat Grey knows better than to lie to me," my father said.

I caught a sparkle of laughter in Meg's eyes as she served the wine, but she wasn't looking at me, she was swapping glances with my mother. The glances seemed to say something about the foolishness of men. I was sure they couldn't include me in that ... then I wasn't so sure. Women are strange creatures.

At the end of the meal Great-Uncle George pulled out his pipe and went on with his grandfather's story ...

ANTHONY MARSDEN'S STORY

After the Battle of Bosworth Field I expected to be executed. To be honest I was so miserable at the death of Lord Dickon I'd have been happy to join him in Heaven ... or more likely in Hell.

But Henry's victorious soldiers surrounded us, told the foot soldiers to get back to their homes, and held the captains and lords for ransom or punishment.

After two days with nothing but water and dry bread I was taken in front of Henry Tudor himself. I hadn't expected that. I thought he'd be too busy taking control of his new kingdom.

He was a frail young man with a narrow, suspicious face and thin yellow hair like rain-ruined straw. He mumbled through bad teeth and I didn't always understand his Welsh accent. To be honest I was bone weary, and I was

distracted by the creature he had sitting on the back of his chair. It looked like a little wide-eyed man, but someone said it was a creature called a monkey. It chewed on a nut and its bright round eyes seemed fixed on me as it ate and chattered.

"Anthony Marsden?" Henry Tudor said.

"Yes, sire."

I received a sharp prod in the back with a spear and a hissed reminder that he was now King Henry VII. "Yes … Your Grace," I said, but those words stuck in my throat. The man didn't look very kingly in his dark gown and simple fur trim.

"You were in the Tower when the sons of Edward IV disappeared, weren't you?" the new King asked.

What was I supposed to answer? Somebody had clearly told him the truth. If I denied it then he would think me a liar. "If all else fails," Dickon always said, "you may have to tell the truth."

So I told Henry what had happened. He wasn't satisfied, because I couldn't tell him if the boys were alive or dead, but he seemed to accept that only Tyrell and his hench-man knew the truth. After nearly an hour I was fainting with weakness and he allowed me to sit down with some watered wine and some of his own white bread. Then he told me, "You can go back to Marsden Manor and pay me a fine of a thousand crowns. You may not leave that manor unless you have my permission."

"Yes, sire … Your Grace."

He knew I didn't have a thousand crowns and I'd have to sell good farmland, barns and orchards to raise the money. Marsden Manor was pruned like a rich rose bush, cut to the ground. It would grow again. But what hurt was having to hand back Bournmoor Woods to Lord gloating, greedy, pompous, old Birtley.

"If I ever catch you in Bournmoor Woods again, Marsden, I'll string you up for crow food," he said, enjoying returning every word that I'd said to him just two years before.

And, in the years that followed, his fat grinning face taunted me every time we met at a market or a meeting of Durham landowners. It was the price that losers have to pay.

I gave up my wandering and my fighting and became a good, hard-working manager of my estate. It was smaller now, but I had more time to make sure it worked well. My soldiers, freed from the endless wars, were my farmers. I taxed them till they squealed, and robbed them of any grain or sheep or cattle that they tried to hide from me. It was a game. They tried to cheat me – I tried to catch them out and punish them.

And I kept a tight grip on lawbreakers and fined them for every crime. I could have executed more, but I preferred the money. Then I could set them free to rob again and be fined again. I paid my fine to the King and still grew rich.

London was two hundred and fifty miles away it could

have been in India for all I cared.

I could have died quietly as a landowner in a small northern estate and been buried in the churchyard with a stone with my name on it. And when that stone was worn flat by wind and time I'd have been forgotten. But History still had a part for me to play. And it came like a stone from a catapult. Suddenly and unexpectedly.

The messenger who arrived at my door was escorted by four armed men dressed in the King's livery. A self-important young man spoke to me as if I were a peasant in a crowded marketplace. "His Grace requests your presence in London, and I am sent to accompany you into His Grace's presence with great urgency."

"The King wants to see *me*?" I said.

"His Grace does indeed request your ..."

"Yes, yes. I heard all that. What does he *want*?"

The young man raised his chin and reached inside his riding cloak. He pulled out a packet with the King's seal and handed it to me. I invited him to take his men to the kitchens where they'd be fed and said I'd join him there when I'd read the letter.

I read through it and sank weak-kneed on to a bench at the table. The messenger found me there a quarter of an hour later when he came to look for me. "You are unwell, Marsden?"

"I'm ... I'm ... I'm ..." I struggled for words. "The Duke of York. The little Prince in the Tower. He's ... he's alive. He's back in England. He wants his throne from Henry Tudor!" I managed to say.

The young man looked down his thin nose at me and said, "That is what the young man says. Of course, *proving* it is another matter."

"You think he is lying? An impostor pretending to be the Prince? If he's lying, then the King would have his head on a pole on London Bridge! Even if he's telling the truth, then he is risking his life by coming out into the open. What does he say? 'Give me my throne back, Henry. Push off back to Wales!'"

The young man did not smile. "The King takes the threat seriously."

I shook the letter. "So I see. I am one of the few people who can identify the lad. He wants me to go to London and see the boy!"

"So can you leave today?"

"My estate …"

"We will arrange for the King's agent in Durham to take care of that. We'll see him when we stay there tonight."

"What if this character is *not* the real Duke of York?"

"Then the King will be pleased if you would tell the world."

"And if it *is* him?"

"The King would be less pleased," the messenger said in a low voice.

"The King would be less pleased! Less pleased! He'd be furious. He'd probably kill me to keep me quiet!" Then I remembered Lord Dickon's advice. "Only tell the truth if you absolutely have to." If the boy really was the little Duke of York then I could lie and say he wasn't!

I rose stiffly from the bench. "I'll make preparations and be with you in half an hour."

"Twenty minutes," the messenger said. "We want to be in Durham before nightfall."

And so I found myself on the road to London, which I

never thought I'd see again.

King Henry VII was more withered and suspicious than ever. After two years of Henry's company the monkey was more wrinkled and worried than I remembered him. Everyone in Henry's court was dull and drab as he pinched pennies like some gold-grubbing moneylender. The page who stood at the door was dressed in a worn jerkin that was patched with some other material. That material had then been blacked with ink that had faded to dark brown. His shoes were scuffed and worn.

Henry looked up from a table covered with letters and books. "I hear you are a bully and a tyrant in your little patch of land," he said.

"I keep a firm hand on my tenants," I admitted.

"Good. I can't stand milksop landlords. Don't let the peasant farmers get grand ideas. Grind their faces in the mud and keep them there, Marsden. Understand?"

"Yes, Your Grace."

"You have land at Wearmouth, Springwell and Houghton, don't you?" he asked sharply. That was Henry Tudor. He knew about accounts and he knew how much money every man had to within a groat. He was no fighter. Our country was being run by a good little clerk, nothing more.

"I have indeed, Your Grace," I said. "I used to own Bournmoor Woods, but I was forced to give them back to Lord Birtley after Bosworth Field ... and Your Grace's glorious victory."

Henry looked surprised, as if he'd forgotten. He didn't forget things like that. "And you would like to earn your Bournmoor Woods *back* from Birtley?" he asked lightly.

"I'd like nothing more."

He nodded. He clicked his fingers and the page boy crossed the room. He was a thin lad with hair as pale and fine as King Henry's. "Bring us some malmsey wine," Henry Tudor said. His eyes danced with some secret joke.

"You remember Richard of Gloucester had a brother," he said.

"The Duke of Clarence," I said as the page brought us two goblets of wine. "He was drowned in malmsey wine," I said, looking at the liquid in my goblet. "I don't suppose this is wine from the barrel he was drowned in?"

Henry fixed his eyes on me and said, "Your dear Richard of Gloucester drowned his own brother Clarence in a barrel of malmsey ... but he didn't drown Clarence's son, Edward of Warwick, did he?"

"No," I said.

"So Edward of Warwick could come and claim the crown from me!" he said quietly.

"He could," I agreed.

"That's why I have Edward of Warwick safely locked up in the Tower of London!" he said with a chuckle so harsh that it set the monkey chattering with fright.

"Imagine my surprise when a young lad appeared and said that *he* was the real Edward of Warwick! When I said that Warwick was in the Tower then the boy changed his story ... now he claims to be the little Duke of York!"

"The young Prince in the Tower!" I said.

"The younger of the two Princes in the Tower," the King agreed. "Your Richard of Gloucester has a sister, Margaret. She's backed this story of the boy – probably gave him some lessons in all the things that the Duke of York would know. Of course the boy is just some sort of puppet the people behind him are much more dangerous. They sent a rebel force across from Ireland to drive me off my throne."

I nodded. "I'd heard there'd been a battle at Stoke. But your forces won, didn't they?"

"Aye, Marsden. Massacred the traitors and captured the boy," he said. A little colour came to his parchment cheeks as he remembered it with pleasure. "The boy who calls himself the Duke of York is in my power. The little Duke of York was guarded in the Tower by you and Will Slaughter. Slaughter has disappeared. The Constable of the Tower, Brackenbury, was killed at Bosworth Field with Richard. That James Tyrell is safely out of reach in France. But I still have you, Marsden," he said.

"For what?" I asked.

"You could recognize the boy. You guarded him for a month or so until Tyrell came and took him away ... or murdered him," he went on.

"He'll have grown and changed," I said.

"Not all that much in four years, Marsden," the King snapped. "So, tell me, have you seen the Duke of York since you came to the palace today?"

"Is this some sort of trick?" I asked.

"Of course!" Henry Tudor said sourly. "If I showed you a boy and said 'Is this the Duke of York?' you might say 'Yes' because you are part of the plot! So have you seen the Duke of York, the little Prince in the Tower, since you came into the palace?"

I thought about it and then shook my head slowly. "No."

Henry leaned back, took the monkey from the back of the chair and stroked it while it wrapped its miniature hands around his finger and tried to bite him. He looked

at the shabby page boy who was standing by the door waiting to serve us more wine. "So, if that boy says he is the Duke of York, he is lying?"

I peered closely at the lad. He was the right age and his fair hair was the right colour, but he was nothing like the happy little duke with whom I'd practised archery in the Tower.

Henry looked at the boy. "Do you know who our visitor is?" he asked, nodding towards me. The blue-eyed boy turned to look at me. He knew it was a test and that he should recognize me. "That's one of my father's friends," he said, "but I can't remember his name."

Henry spoke slowly. "It is not. You are a liar. You are not the Duke of Warwick and you are not the Duke of York. I should have your simple little head removed and stuck on a pole as an example to other dreamers who want to take my throne. But I will not. You can go and work in my kitchen, my little prince of patches!"

The boy looked defeated and dejected. He turned and walked out of the door. "You brought me to London to identify this fraud?" I asked.

"I did," Henry said calmly. "It is just possible that the Princes in the Tower escaped – unlikely, but just possible. I wanted to be quite, quite sure. You have taken a weight off my mind, Marsden, and I'd like to give you a gift!" he said.

"A gift?"

"Yes. I want to give you Bournmoor Woods again, my little tyrant of Marsden Manor."

"Thank you, Your Grace!" I said. "You are very generous."

"Not really," he said with a shrug. "You make more money and will pay better taxes than Birtley does for that miserable patch of land."

"I will?"

"Twenty pounds a year," he said.

"It's worth just ten."

He looked at me. "But think of Birtley's face when you tell him! That must be worth ten pounds a year!"

"Priceless," I grinned.

"Then I'll charge you fifty pounds a year," he said.

"Not that priceless," I said. I felt the grin slide from my face.

He bent his head over the book in front of him, picked up a quill and began to scrawl a permit for me to take possession of the woods. He held it out and I took it with a bow before backing towards the door. His queen entered as I was leaving, their baby son Arthur in her arms. I bowed low to her and caught a glimpse of her shoes. The gossips in the palace said the Queen wore buckles of tin because the King was too mean to buy her silver. Her gowns were mended time and time again, frayed cuffs turned up and worn threads patched.

They also said she had to borrow money from her servants. It wasn't only the unknown kitchen boy who was a miserable thing of rags and patches.

Richard was a hard and cruel man, but he had been "alive". Henry had cold water for blood and a shrivelled walnut for a heart. Richard's gifts were freely given and generous. Henry's gift had cost me ten pounds a year!

I rode back to Marsden Manor with little thought for the pathetic boy who said he was the Duke of York. I was a happier and a richer man. I thought the story of the Princes was finally over.

I was wrong.

CHAPTER FOURTEEN

"Dream on, dream on, of bloody deeds and death"

Great-Uncle George tapped his pipe on the fireplace. "It turned out that the boy was called Lambert Simnel. They said his father was a joiner from Oxford. Goodness knows how he hoped to get away with the trick!"

"Because the people who used the boy were fools." Grandmother stopped sucking on a rabbit bone and cut in. "The boy was lucky to get away with his life!"

"I don't know," Grandfather sighed. "King Henry sounds like a very sensible young man. Careful with his money. He got himself an extra kitchen boy free! Why can't we do that, James? The servants here cost us almost five pounds a year ... and we feed them *and* we give them shelter."

"Aye," Meg whispered, "in the attic with the bats and the beetles."

My mother said softly, "We spend less on the household than any other manor I know of. I had thought we could pay them *more* ..."

"More!" Grandfather exploded. "When I was a lad Henry VIII fixed servants' wages at three pounds for four years' work – and women were paid three pounds every six years, of course."

"Of course," Meg murmured.

"It's time we cut their wages again," Grandfather went on. "They're rogues anyway."

Meg was sitting at my feet out of sight of the others, and I saw her knuckles turn pale as she gripped the arm of my chair tight to hold in her anger. I thought she was going to make some enraged reply so I rose from my chair and said, "That reminds me. I need to see if Martin the Ostler has found me a saddle!" I nudged Meg with my knee to follow me out of the room.

"At this time of night?" my father was saying.

"Let him go," said my mother.

The dark corridor at the back of the house was almost lit up by Meg's glowing rage. "Why are the rich so mean?" she asked.

"That's why they're rich," I told her. "They take extra care of their money."

"Then they shouldn't be surprised when the poor try to rob them," she said.

I stepped out of the back door and into the stable yard. The cold wind was rattling leaves around the paved yard and making a lantern swing wildly on a hook by the stable door. I crossed and looked at the grey horse. I patted its muzzle and thought about its murdered master. "We still don't know who he is," I said.

Meg had calmed a little and said, "You're right. A man shouldn't be buried without a name. Even if he is a thief."

"I want to look at his clothes ... and I want to find his saddle," I said.

Meg's hair was blowing free so that it was practically covering her face. From somewhere in the mass of hair she said, "The Princes in the Tower died because of who they were and what they were."

"Yes," I said. "So?"

"So ... maybe the stranger died because of *who* he was and *what* he was," she said. "If we know *who* he was we may be able to work out *what* he was. Then we may know why he died ... and then we can work out who killed him!"

"The clothes were in the other saddle-bag," I said. "We looked at the letters, but we didn't examine the other pouch. There may be some secret in there."

"It's a good place to start," she nodded.

We followed the paths round the fringe of Bournmoor Woods till we reached the small cottage again. Meg's steps were so certain I felt she must be able to see in the dark like a cat. Then I remembered that the Devil appears to witches as a cat, and decided not to accuse her of having a cat's eyes. I'd seen what she'd done to Wat Grey in the stocks and knew she wasn't a girl to upset too often.

It was still early evening and the old woman was grinding herbs in a bowl when Meg pushed open the door. "Hello, Meg," Widow Atkinson said. "I knew you'd be

back. You won't give up on this mystery until it's solved, will you?"

"No, Mrs Atkinson," Meg said.

We edged into the house. With just three of us there it seemed crowded. At least it was warm in the glow of the turf fire after the chill, damp air that blew from the woods.

"You'll be wanting to look in the other pouch of the saddle-bag, I expect."

I was disturbed that the woman knew what we wanted before we had even asked. But Meg didn't seem at all surprised. "That's right."

"Of course, Magistrate Marsden came and took the body this morning."

"I know," Meg said.

"And he also took the saddle-bag."

"So we can't see what was in it."

"Important letters were missing, he said."

"But there were clothes in the other side, weren't there?" I asked.

"There were."

"Did Father take those away too?" I asked.

"He did," the old woman said. She looked up, her faded eyes shining in the light of the tallow candle with some amusing secret.

Meg guessed it first. "But you looked inside first, didn't you, Mrs Atkinson?"

The woman placed a hand on her heart as if she was shocked at the thought. "They simply fell out on the floor," she said. "I hardly glanced at them as I put them back."

Meg nodded patiently. "Of course not, Mrs Atkinson.

But there was something curious about the clothes, wasn't there?"

The woman looked across and met the girl's gaze. "If you get any sharper, Meg Lumley, you'll cut yourself."

"So what did you find?" I cried, not enjoying their slow game of wits.

The woman wiped her hands on her apron and looked at me. "I found some clothes that would fit a large man – the size of the murdered man. They were mostly clean and freshly washed and rinsed in rosewater. But one dirty shirt had long fair hair clinging to the collar."

"Ah!" Meg exclaimed.

"So what?" I asked.

"Don't you see what this means?" Meg cried.

"No."

"Then you need lessons in thinking, not lessons in reading!" she said spitefully.

Before I could reply Widow Atkinson said, "And, talking about reading, Master Marsden, perhaps you can tell me what this means?"

The woman took some herbs and sprinkled them on the table. They made three lines in the shape of "H".

"This letter was embroidered on a piece of the man's linen," she explained. "I couldn't understand it, but I remembered the shape."

"It's an aitch," I said.

"A what?" Meg asked.

"An aitch – the letter aitch!"

"Ah," she said as if she were a little disappointed.

Widow Atkinson looked across the table at me. "Your father has the saddle-bag, he has the clothes, he has the body ... he has everything he needs to solve the mystery."

"Except the letters and the dead man's horse," Meg said.

"Ah, yes," the woman agreed. "But William here will have told his father about the letters and the horse."

"Er ... no. Not yet," I confessed.

"Then go back and tell him at once!" Widow Atkinson urged. "It's a day since the murder, and the killer will be eager to get on his way. He'll be worried that the spirit of the dead man will come back to haunt him if he stays too near the place of death."

"Richard III was haunted at Bosworth Field even though the Princes died in the Tower of London," I told her.

"Some crimes have longer shadows than others," she said.

"So you know who killed the stranger?" I asked. "Tell me!"

Widow Atkinson turned back to her herbs, "I'm accused of witchcraft in this village," she said. "All I'm guilty of is using a bit of sense. If I tell you who killed the stranger then you'll go saying it's witchcraft. Use your own sense – and the sense of your friend Meg Lumley – and you can come to the same answer. But I won't say anything that might end up with me being ducked in the Wear as a witch, you understand?"

I looked at Meg. "So you know who the killer is?"

She frowned. "I thought I did. But that 'aitch' thing has muddled me. I need to think again. Maybe we can go to the Black Bull and talk about it."

"The tavern!" I exclaimed. "Michael will throw us out."

"Not if you have some money in your purse," she said.

She turned to the door and said, "Goodnight, Mrs Atkinson."

"One moment, child!" Widow Atkinson reached on to the shelf and took down a small glass bottle. "Remember, you're hunting a killer. A man with ice in his veins, who will kill you if he has to just as he'd kill a wasp that bothered him."

"I'll be careful," Meg promised.

"Try to drop some of this in his food or drink," the woman advised.

"Will it kill him?" Meg asked.

"No, but it will make him sleep for at least a few hours. It would only kill him if he drank the whole bottle. But while he's asleep you can overpower him and hand him over to the magistrate."

The girl slipped the bottle into a bag that hung from her belt. "Come on, William," she said, stepping out into the autumn night. "Let's go to the Black Bull."

Her feet stepped lightly over the puddles and the stones as we headed for the village. The tavern sign rattled over the door and we stepped into the thick, stinking air and

into the roar of noise. Men shouted, argued and laughed. Women's voices cried over the top of them, shrieked with laughter or complained and bickered. I had no idea the people of the village spent their evenings like this. Serving maids pushed through the crowd to serve greasy stew on platters and slopped jugs of ale on to the crowded tables.

We squeezed into a corner and a maid with a white, wine-stained apron took an order for a jug of ale and two mugs. When it arrived it was cloudy brown and soupy with dregs. Michael the Taverner's customers didn't appear too fussy. I paid the woman from my purse and half a dozen pairs of eyes watched me as I slipped it inside my doublet. Then the eyes slid away as if they had no interest in my money at all.

Wat Grey sat across the room from us. From time to time the crowds parted so we could see across to him. His look was as dark and poisonous as nightshade. "He's in partnership with Michael the Taverner," I said to Meg.

"That's right," she agreed. "Wat Grey steals the horses – or buys them from horse-priggers. Michael lets him use the stables at the back of the Black Bull here to work on them. He can dye them or paint them before he sells them on. Michael takes a share of the profit."

"He does more than that," a voice said.

I hadn't realized we'd been talking so loudly as to be heard over the noise of the crowd. Constable Smith had sat beside me while I'd been turned towards Meg and had heard everything. "What was that, Constable?" I said.

"A tavern is the perfect place to sell horses. Especially a tavern on the Wearmouth to Newcastle road like this. Travellers stop here and may need a fresh horse. Michael says, 'I just happen to have one in my stables for sale.'"

The smith breathed ale-fumes in my face and the smell of the charcoal smoke stung my nose. "He even makes sure they need a new horse – he hobbles the horse that a visitor arrives on. Wat Grey has a trick with a cord that makes the horse go lame overnight. Next morning the traveller finds his horse is not sound enough to ride. So he exchanges it for Wat's stolen horse – plus some cash. The stolen horse is fifty miles away by nightfall and Wat has a good horse in his stable. And it's a legal horse. He can sell it at Houghton mart."

"It's a lame horse," I say.

"No, no! The cord trick leaves it lame for just a few hours. It's as fit as a foal by the time it gets to mart!" he explained.

"So why don't you arrest him?" I demanded. "You're the constable."

His large face came close to mine. His eyes had a damp film over them and I realized he'd been drinking heavily. That was probably the only reason he was telling me this. "I'm only a village constable," he said. "This is a huge trade, all over the north of England. Arresting Wat Grey wouldn't stop it. Arresting Michael the Taverner wouldn't stop it! It's hard to prove a horse has been stolen when it could have come from York or Carlisle or Hexham or Whitby."

"Hanging one of the horse thieves might stop them from coming here," I argued. I felt Meg press my hand in warning, but I went on, "You may not bother about horse thieves, but you should be bothered about a murder in Bournmoor Woods!" My voice was getting loud and I thought maybe Michael's muddy ale was overheating my brain too.

"The killer in Bournmoor Woods is in the next county by now!" the smith said. "Some horse thief went for the horse, but killed the man by mistake and rode off in a panic."

"Without the horse?" I said.

The smith suddenly looked sober. "Aye … I'd heard you found the horse."

"So why shouldn't Wat Grey or Michael the Taverner be the killer?" I cried. Heads were turning towards us now. I could see no faces clearly, only a fuzzy blur of red-cheeked women and coarse-shaven men. The faces that were missing were those of Wat Grey and Michael the Taverner. I wondered where they'd gone.

"I can't prove they're guilty," the constable said. "And you can't prove they're guilty."

"And they can't prove they're innocent!" I argued. I felt pleased with my cleverness.

"You'd hang them because they can't prove they're innocent!" he said. "That's just what your father would do. But even he can't do that. Do you know why?"

"No!" I said, suddenly confused by the switch of his argument.

"Because he'd have to hang himself! He couldn't prove *he's* innocent either!" the smith sneered. Now there was no doubt the rest of the customers in the tavern were taking an interest in our argument.

"He was in Marsden Manor when the murder was reported," I said. "You saw him yourself!"

"Pah!" He spat a spray of ale and spittle in my face. "But where was he when the murder took place? That's a different matter altogether! He could have killed the stranger, hidden the body and ridden back to Marsden Manor."

It was true that Wat Grey had seen a dark-cloaked stranger ride away, but Wat could have been lying. There was a buzzing in my head as if a bee had crawled in and couldn't get out. "My father had no reason to kill a stranger."

"Hah!" The blacksmith laughed and sprayed me again. "The letters. There were secret letters in that saddle-bag when Wat Grey found it with the body. But he left them there. Your father went to see the body this morning and those letters aren't there now! He took them!"

"No, he didn't!" I cried. "Because I've got ..."

"Because I've got ... to be going now!" Meg cut in. She grabbed my arm with surprising strength and hauled me to my feet. It's hard to stand straight when the room is swaying unsteadily. Maybe the autumn wind was rocking it.

"Find the letters and you find the murderer!" Constable Smith shouted.

"Aye!" someone in the taproom agreed loudly. The crowd was muttering something about the "miserable Marsdens" and hands were resting on daggers as Meg dragged me towards the door.

"I know who the murderer is!" I called as Meg hauled me closer to the door, using her sharp elbows to make her way through the angry crowd.

"No, he doesn't!" she cried. "He's drunk! Ignore him!"

"I'm not drunk!" I said, struggling against her grip on my arm.

"Of course you're drunk," she hissed. "Get outside!" With a final push she sent me through the door, on to the muddy path where I found myself looking down into the ripples of a puddle. I retched and threw up my ale into the muddy water.

I felt as if I were dying. But the door swung open and light spilled out on to the roadway. People began to follow us. Meg's hand was on my collar, dragging me back to my feet and down the road towards Marsden Manor.

I spent as much time on my hands and knees as I did on my feet as I crawled back home. "It's Smith!" I said. "Constable Smith's the killer! Grey and Michael the Taverner know that. He's protecting their horse-thieving and they're protecting his murder! They're all in it together!"

"I know that!" Meg snapped. "*Everybody* knows that Constable Smith is in league with Wat and Michael ... everybody knows it except your stupid father. But if the killer really *is* one of those three then you've just given him a very good reason for wanting *you* dead!"

I stopped and leaned against the doorpost of the house. "Oh," I said.

"Get inside, sit in a dark corner at the side of the fireplace and dry out ... and sober up," she ordered as she pushed me into the dining hall. The family hardly noticed me. They were too busy listening to Great-Uncle George, who was standing with his back to the fire and talking.

CHAPTER FIFTEEN

"Advance your standards, draw your willing swords"

"I'm sure King James VI of Scotland is a good ruler, and a wise man," he was saying.

"Wise? And a man?" Grandmother cackled. "There's a rare thing!"

I shivered, felt dizzy and sick, yet it was a comfort being back in my own home listening to the familiar snapping. Only Humphrey Vere seemed to notice I was there. His face was serious and that "V" on his top lip looked sharper and crueller than ever. He smiled when he saw Meg settle next to me and I could see I was wrong about the man.

"What I am saying," Great-Uncle George went on heavily, "is that no matter how clever he is, he is still a Scot."

"So what?" Grandmother said.

"No, a Scot," Great-Uncle George teased. "Now, those folk in the south of England hate us folk in the north ... always have, always will. And we hate the Scots – we've had to live with their raiding and their thieving for a thousand years – ever since Hadrian's Wall stopped keeping them out! But the big problem is, Master Vere, that the people in the south of England don't hate the Scots. The folk in London don't have to live next door to them, so they haven't had to deal with them."

"People always have problems with their neighbours," Grandmother nodded in rare agreement.

"Exactly!" Great-Uncle George said. "The lords down in London may want James as their next king – up in the north we're not so sure! Do you want him, Master Vere?" he asked suddenly.

"Why ... why, I have been trusted with taking the letters to him. The Queen and Secretary Cecil trust me," he said. I noticed that he hadn't answered Great-Uncle George's question.

"Last night I was saying that when a king dies there's always trouble. But it's strange, you know, that the trouble often comes from Scotland!"

"Earlier tonight you told us about the first Tudor. I seem to remember he came from Wales!" Grandfather sniffed.

"Ah, but the first attacks on Henry Tudor's throne came from Scotland! A young man claiming to be the Duke of York – the little Prince in the Tower – turned to the old enemy north of the border for help."

Humphrey Vere leaned forward. "But, Sir George – you told us this morning the attack came from Ireland!"

"Ah! That was Lambert Simnel – the Oxford boy. The *first* Pretender. But the *second* one was even more dangerous. His name was Perkin Warbeck. If he'd succeeded, then the Scots would be ruling England already! Because he went to James IV of Scotland for help. Luckily Henry Tudor had my grandfather to defend England against the new attacker."

"I thought our grandfather fought against Henry Tudor," Grandmother complained.

"He did ... at Bosworth Field. But when an attack comes from the north we are fighting for Marsden Manor and life itself. You'd fight for the Devil himself if it meant saving your family and your estate!"

And Great-Uncle George told his grandfather's last story ...

ANTHONY MARSDEN'S STORY

For four years we'd had peace. Marsden Manor grew richer and stronger. I was able to buy new lands on the Tyne and a town house in Durham. And on one of my visits to torment my dear Lord Birtley I discovered his daughter, Isabel, had blossomed into a fine young woman. She had a sparkling eye and was looking at me with interest.

Of course Lord Birtley was furious and refused to let me even speak to Isabel. But he died suddenly and her brother took over as head of the family. Nothing stood in our way then and we married.

Now, this has nothing to do with my story, you understand, but I missed Lord Birtley as much as I missed my lord Dickon. Life seemed empty for a while when I didn't have him to hate!

However, Isabel and I settled in Marsden Manor and led a busy life but a quiet one. We were still getting news from London and Henry Tudor still had problems. If any enemy of the King wanted to start trouble, then they dug up the old story of the Princes in the Tower. The Princes were still alive, they said.

Every year around springtime the trees in Bournmoor Woods began to bud, the roads dried up and someone made the trip north to see me. "What do you know about the Princes in the Tower?" they wanted to know. Had I seen their bodies? No. Could they have escaped alive? Yes. Did I know where they went? No.

But in 1492, nearly nine years after I'd last seen the little Duke of York, he turned up in Flanders. Dickon's own sister, Margaret, recognized him even though he was almost eighteen years old by then! She said she would back him if he wanted to invade England and take Henry Tudor's crown.

I had an odd stirring in my bones. I wanted to brush the rust off my armour and maybe help the lad. But Isabel stopped me. "We have peace. Leave it that way."

"But this lad would be the rightful king if he was the Duke of York!" I argued.

"Who says?"

"Dickon's sister," I told her.

"She *would* say that, wouldn't she? Anything to get revenge on Henry Tudor, who killed her brother and took his crown. No, King Henry is a firm, fair king …"

"And a mean little man," I muttered.

"A fair, firm king," she repeated. "What happened to Marsden Manor last time you fought against him?"

"I lost a lot of land," I said miserably. Isabel was right. I hated it when she was right.

"You lost a lot of land and you nearly lost your life. Sooner or later you have to settle down, Anthony. Decide to fight for the King and stick with the King."

"But I don't like him. He's not as *good* as Richard III," I argued.

She looked at me over the top of her embroidery frame, the way she did, and said, "He's the best king we've got."

I sighed. My heart went out to the young Duke of York.

But Isabel was in my heart too – and she had spoken what was in my head.

Henry Tudor wasn't sitting back and waiting for the invasion. He rounded up Perkin Warbeck's supporters in England and locked them away. The most dangerous ones, like one of the Stanley family, lost their treacherous heads. Now that wouldn't have stopped me supporting Perkin Warbeck if he'd *really* been the Duke of York. My lord Dickon had died fighting Henry Tudor and I didn't mind dying the same way, no matter what Isabel said. But what finally decided me to settle for Henry Tudor was Perkin Warbeck's next move.

He landed in Scotland!

James IV offered to help the lad, and messages went all around the north telling us to arm ourselves and get ready for an invasion. Suddenly I forgot all my doubts about Henry Tudor. I detested the cold, mean, grasping little horn-thumb. But I was *more* afraid of the Scots.

James IV would attack all right. But if he defeated Henry Tudor he wouldn't go home. He'd kill Perkin Warbeck and take the throne of England for himself. The men who fought against him would be cut into pieces small enough to feed a cat. Lands like Marsden Manor would be given as a reward to some scrawny Scottish lord, robbed and ruined and left to rot.

I gathered my horse soldiers and foot soldiers on the village green in the summer of 1496 and people came from miles around to watch us training. The men were as rusty as their swords and we'd all lost some of the fire that had driven us to war for Richard eleven years before. But we brought in young men, the smiths worked sixteen hours a day making new chain mail, the weavers made the tabards with the Marsden symbol of St George and the Dragon – pale blue figures on a dark red background. The woods were stripped to make new bows, arrows, pikes and staves.

Messengers sped through to London with the latest news of the Scots' preparations. Soldiers from the south brought cannon up to defend the northern castles at Bamburgh, Alnwick and Newcastle, and traders came in to sell us strong horses fit for a battle.

Rogues and cheats moved in too. Mean King Henry actually sent some money to pay the Marsden Manor men for the work they were missing in the fields. Instead of sheep and corn these men had gold. They went to the Black Bull for a drink after a thirsty day's practice in the summer sun … and lost the gold on the gaming tables to the tricksters.

I had masons build up the walls around Marsden Hall, although I knew that wouldn't keep the Scots out for long if they got this far south. Stone walls kept out men with arrows a hundred years ago, but they were no barrier to men with cannon. We had to beat the Scots on the open battlefield. And we had to march north to meet them as soon as we were ready – not wait for them to march south and catch us like rabbits in our warrens.

By September the spies reported the Scots were moving out of Edinburgh. Ready or not, we had to move north to meet them. The men from Durham gathered at Gateshead and crossed the Tyne in a colourful procession that took half an hour to pass through the twisting streets of the town and out on to the Northumberland moors.

I enjoyed riding with Isabel's brother, the young Lord Birtley, and treated him to tales of the battles I'd fought

with my lord Dickon. "It's strange. Thirteen years ago I was riding south to lay hands on the Prince of Wales. Now I'm riding north to lay my hands on his younger brother. Of course, then we were riding dressed in black and the local people weren't too friendly. I think we'll find the people of this county treat us more like saviours than invaders!"

And, at Morpeth where we rested the first night, we were certainly welcomed by excited and cheering crowds. War almost felt worth fighting. But the thought of dying, and leaving Isabel alone and undefended, took some of the sweetness out of that ride. "You're growing old, Marsden," I told myself.

In three days we sighted the smoke on the skyline. The Scots, in their usual way, began burning and looting the villages they passed through as soon as they crossed the border. Our scouts came back that night and said the Scots weren't a single, massed army. They were a dozen raiding parties in a scattered line, heading south.

Our commander was the Duke of Northumberland who'd joined us at Alnwick. The Duke said, "The problem is they are heading south down at least six routes. If we stop one, then the other five slip past us. If we spread ourselves, then we may be outnumbered."

"One Englishman is worth ten Scots, so that can't happen!" someone cried. His call was met with cheers and laughter.

I stepped forward. "I've fought the Scots before," I said. "They form their foot soldiers into a packed square and let our horsemen ride into a steel hedge of spears. We can break up their square if we have enough archers – but we haven't."

"So how do we fight them?" the Duke asked.

"We don't," I told him. "We let them fight us. The Scots aren't so good when they have to go forward and attack. They don't have the organization we've been working on for the past month. They charge wildly forward and we can pick them off one man at a time. All we need to do is to stand firm."

The Duke looked pleased. "There you are! You've heard the word of a man who fought at Bosworth Field!"

"Aye, but he was on the losing side!" someone jeered.

Ten years before I would have probably killed him. Now I just smiled. "Now I've joined the winning side."

So, with my battle plan agreed, we split into six groups and headed for strong positions that would block the Scottish advances. I led my group to a hill top overlooking the road to Wooler. Scouts reported that our Scots enemy were camped just five miles away. And their banner carried a white rose of York on it. Tomorrow we would be facing the Duke of York himself ... or Perkin

Warbeck.

"It's like Ambien Hill," I said to Birtley in our tent that night.

"Where?"

He was young. Only eleven years had passed and already memories were dying. "At Bosworth Field," I explained. "Richard sat on Ambien Hill. He'd have survived if he hadn't charged down."

Birtley nodded. "King Harold sat on Senlac Hill at the Battle of Hastings – and he'd have beaten the Normans if he hadn't charged down. I'll make sure the men know how important it is."

Birtley was a good lad. Clever as his sister. I felt that this was a battle we couldn't lose. That night I slept soundly. I had none of Richard's nightmares on the eve of Bosworth Field ... but then I hadn't arranged the murder of my two young nephews.

I fell asleep thinking. Richard couldn't have ordered the deaths of his young nephews if the young man on the other side of the hill was really my lively little Duke of York. I hoped I didn't have to kill him.

The morning was misty and the dewy air muffled the sound of men getting ready for the battle. For many of them it was their first battle ... for some it would be their last. They all went about their business in a quiet sober mood.

I placed a small group of men on the road to block the Scots advance. The rest of the men were drawn up on the hillside in full view of the road. The Scots would know that as soon as they tried to advance against the men on the road they would be crushed by the horsemen charging down from the hill.

The first thing we saw over the crest of the hill was the black banner with the white rose. There were about a thousand men marching behind the banner and perhaps a hundred on horseback. We had fewer men but more horses.

The Scots stopped in a ragged line. Their leaders gathered in a group and looked towards our banners as if to read them. Then one horseman, a young man in armour, rode forward. A bodyguard of two knights rode on either side of him. The rest of the army relaxed and settled back on the grass that was drying quickly in the September sunshine.

I mounted my horse and rode slowly forward to meet the party of three. I had young Birtley at my side. When we were ten paces from the Scots we stopped. The young man took off his helmet and shook down his fine fair hair.

"Anthony Marsden," he said. His voice was soft and his accent had just a hint of the Flemish tongue.

"You read that from my banners," I said.

He gave a wide smile. "No, my old friend, I read it from your face."

"We've met?" I asked.

"Don't you remember me? It's been thirteen years and

I've changed … but then I was just a nine-year-old boy. You've changed less."

Oh, but he was good, this Perkin Warbeck. He knew where the little Duke of York had met Anthony Marsden of Marsden Manor, and he was using that knowledge. "Thank you, my lord," I said. I shouldn't have called him "my lord" but the words slipped out.

He allowed himself a small smile. "You were good to me in the Tower, Marsden. You and Will Slaughter."

"Was I?"

"Oh, yes. You let us out to practise our archery. You never treated us like prisoners," he went on.

I felt a giddiness that was nothing to do with the sun making me sweat in my padded armour. This youth of twenty-two just could be the Duke of York … and my lord Dickon could be innocent of the murders. "I'm glad you thought so," I said. It was a foolish thing to say. It was admitting I believed him. But my heart was making words my brain didn't want to say.

"I've remembered you with kindness, Marsden. I will reward you well when I've taken the crown off Henry Tudor."

"You think you can do that?"

"With your help!" the young man said.

"My help?"

"Oh, yes. You'll not only let your rightful king pass by on this road – you will also join me on the march against the little Welshman."

And I was tempted. I was blinded by the soft words, the promises, the memories and the miracle of seeing a dead child grown up into a man. It was up to my friend Birtley to save me. "What happened to your brother, the Prince of Wales?" he asked.

"We escaped with the help of Sir Robert Brackenbury, the Constable of the Tower," the youth explained. "But my brother Edward died on the sea voyage. I miss him to this day. He was always so cheerful. He kept me going through those days of imprisonment in the Tower."

He shouldn't have said that. Perkin Warbeck was a liar – a good liar, but a liar. And like so many liars he *had* to tell one lie too many. Edward, Prince of Wales, was miserable and desperate when he was in the Tower.

The mists of memory cleared from my eyes. The young man didn't really look like my little Duke of York. I looked at Birtley and gave a tiny shake of my head. "Go back to Scotland, Warbeck," I said. "We will let you live if you turn back now."

The confident smile vanished. "I'm the Duke of York. Your king!"

"You are Perkin Warbeck, a fraud and a pretender."

The young man nudged his horse forward so he was out of earshot of the two knights. "Listen, Marsden. I can't go back! These men are looting and burning. They're out of control! If I ever get to London I won't be able to handle them!"

"You won't have to," I said coldly. "They'll murder you."

"That's what I think now!" he said, his voice a whine. "Take me with you, Marsden. Take me with you."

I was disappointed. Just for a moment I wanted the Prince in the Tower to have lived. Now he was dead – killed all over again. I was bitter. "Go back to Scotland, Warbeck," I said. I turned my horse and rode slowly back to my men.

The dejected figure, shoulders slumped, turned and rode back to the Scots where they waited on the soft verges of the road. They sprang to their feet, ready to do battle. But after the captains met again there was a shouting of orders and a waving of arms. The Scots army turned and began to trudge back to where they had come from. The warriors gave many backward glances as if they wished they could turn their steel against the hated old enemy. But there was to be no battle for us that day.

"And no battles ever again, Anthony," my wife said, when I returned to Marsden Manor a week later.

"We can't always decide when we want to fight," I told her. "But there'll be no more war for me ... if I can help it."

That seemed to satisfy her. She'd done something two kings had failed to do. She'd made me into a peaceful man.

CHAPTER SIXTEEN

"Lord, Lord! Methought what pain it was to drown"

My Great-Uncle George stopped and looked around the family gathered there. He stroked the coat of arms on the chimney breast. "She probably spoke those very words standing here ... or sitting where you are, Marion."

"That's right," Grandmother retorted. "You can be sure Anthony Marsden would have been standing at the fire. Blocking all the warmth from the womenfolk!"

"And what happened to this Perkin Warbeck?" my father demanded. "You can't end the story there, Uncle George."

"Perkin Warbeck was captured two years later. Just like Lambert Simnel before him he was allowed into the King's royal palace. But Perkin was a fool. He tried to escape. That's when Henry had him locked in the Tower."

"Serve him right if he ended up in the same cell as the real Prince of Wales," Grandfather chuckled nastily. "You should never rebel against your king. That Henry VII seems to have been a very sound chap."

"Careful with his money," Grandmother said with a voice as sharp as acid. "Just like you."

"That's what I said," Grandfather nodded, not quite understanding. "A sound chap."

Great-Uncle George went on. "People saw Warbeck

a year after he'd been imprisoned. They say he had aged ten years. The Tower was killing him as surely as it killed the Princes. He tried to escape again and this time Henry Tudor had to have him executed. He was hanged at Tyburn after he admitted he wasn't really the Duke of York."

"Hanged?" my father said. "Not beheaded?"

"No," Grandfather said with a sigh. "You are a magistrate. You should know better than that. Common criminals are hanged. Only people of noble birth have the honour of the axe!"

"Of course," my father muttered. "I forget, he wasn't who he said he was."

I gave a gasp. I couldn't help myself. The family turned towards me and Humphrey Vere's sharp eyes fixed me in my quiet corner.

My head had cleared of the thick ale. And everything else was cleared. "He wasn't who he said he was!" I whispered. "That's the answer!" And pieces fell into place like bits of armour. Separately they were no use, but put all those bits together in the right order and you have the figure of an armoured man. Or, in my case, I had the figure of a murderer.

I pushed backwards so the wall would support me and struggled to my feet. "Sorry!" I gasped. "I need some fresh air."

I walked unsteadily towards the hall door and out into the cold night. I wanted to talk to Meg about it – or even Mrs Atkinson. But first I had to get it straight in my own mind. I ran through the murder in my thoughts, from Humphrey Vere leaving York to the murdered man being taken to Widow Atkinson's hut. There was just one explanation that fitted the facts. All I had to do now was tell the right people to have the murderer arrested, to deliver the letters safely to James, and to save my country from another war with Scotland.

I was standing at the gateway to Marsden Manor. The walls were high as ever – my Great-Great-Grandfather Anthony Marsden's walls – but the gates were rarely closed now. They were usually left open, even at night.

Tattered clouds drifted across the quarter-moon and sometimes allowed enough light to sparkle on the muddy puddles in the road. They also allowed enough light for someone to see me standing there.

Of course the gate had been open. Any of the mob who'd followed me from the village could have been hiding in the garden. The angry Michael the Taverner, the vengeful Wat Grey, or the devious Constable Smith.

I'd forgotten about the way they'd driven me from the village. If I'd seen them marching up the road I would not have been surprised. But I was surprised when the attack came from behind me. There was a soft rustle, and the

moonlight vanished as the coarse sack was dragged over my head and pulled down to my feet.

The hands that gripped me were strong. They would be. They had strangled the rider in the forest with no trouble at all. They couldn't strangle me. They would never get away with a second murder. I spat sacking from my mouth and cried, "Help!" but an iron fist punched me in the back of the head and knocked me out.

When I woke from my daze I remembered I was inside the sack, but my head seemed to be pointing downwards and it was hurting. My stomach was being pressed and I wanted to vomit the last of the ale, but with my head in that position I feared I'd choke. As my head cleared I realized I was being carried, slung over someone's shoulder. I knew it was the killer, and I knew there would be no mercy for me.

As Great-Uncle George said, "It's not the hot-tempered men you need to worry about – it's the cold-blooded ones." And this one had calculated the first murder as my grandfather calculated the moneys we earned from every acre of Marsden Manor. He hadn't calculated that I would see through his trickery, but it was no problem to a man like that. He would simply take me out of the calculation.

As I bounced along I heard the sound of his feet on the path and branches pushed against me. I guessed we were going through Bournmoor Woods. The man's steps seemed long and jarred me. I guessed we were heading towards the river.

I wondered how he'd do it. Maybe strangle me the way he had strangled the horseman. Maybe he'd stab me to make it look like a theft, the way he'd tried to make the last one look. Then the footsteps slowed and there was the rattle of loose boards beneath me. I was put down on my feet and leaned forward. I felt some sort of rail under my aching stomach.

I was on the footbridge over the River Wear. I'd fished here when I was younger. The river took a sharp turn and the water here was still and deep. Then I knew what he planned and I knew I'd never go fishing again. Not here. Not anywhere.

He seemed to be checking that the sack was tied firmly under my feet. The dust in the sack was choking me and mixing with spittle in my mouth to taste like uncooked bread. Of course this was a flour sack and I was chewing on my last supper.

Suddenly the bottom of the sack was raised and I toppled forward. I stretched my hands above my head as if I were trying to make the fall into a dive. I hit the water with the back of my neck. There was a sudden jolt as I stopped falling, then the cold, clammy clutch of water seeping through on to my face. It was like a sharp slap and it seemed to wake my mind. I knew what I had to do.

The water was creeping through my clothes. It was so cold it stopped my breathing. As the water began to trickle into my mouth I realized I had to close it and hold my breath. I had been quite free inside the sack when I was being carried, but now the wet flour was pasting it to my body, making it cling and stopping my movement.

Still I pulled my hand down to my belt and clutched at my right hip. Nothing there! I panicked for a moment then moved my hand quickly backwards and forwards. The leather sheath had slipped round to my back. I snatched at the handle of my knife, slid it out and turned it so it was pointing away from me.

Now my lungs were beginning to burn. Now they were

telling me to open my mouth and let in air. They hadn't the sense to know they'd be letting in damp death. The knife was razor sharp, but still it was slow in cutting through the wet sacking that moved away as I stabbed at it. At last I pushed through with the knife in my right hand and held the sack firmly with my left as I ripped upwards.

Now there were a million colours in front of my eyes. Jagged shapes of red and blue and yellow, blinding me and distracting me. Those colours were all inside my head and I shook them away. At last the slit in the sacking reached my throat. I felt for the ragged edge with my hands and somehow dropped the knife. It didn't matter. I pushed my head into the slit and pulled down with my hands. Then I used my free hands to pull down on the water and claw towards the surface of the water. The sacking clung to my legs like some giant water eel. I couldn't use my legs to kick upwards, only my hands.

Then the blackness lightened to a faint silver-blue and

my head broke the surface of the water. I wanted to suck in that beautiful air with a gasp of joy, but my mind was working already. He would have dropped me in the river, then hurried away. He had to get back before he was missed. But I'd only been under the water half a minute. He could still be in earshot. If he heard me and came back, he'd make quite sure I was dead before I went in the water next time.

As I sucked in the air the sacking round my legs dragged me back down and I took in half a pint of water before I clawed my way, choking, back to the surface. This time I worked hard with my arms to keep my head above the surface without making too much noise with my thrashing.

The colours were fading in my aching head and the blessed moon came out to show some shapes in the chimney blackness of the overhanging trees. At the foot of the bridge a willow dangled its limp branches into the water. I beat the water with my arms and reached the thin branches with my hands. My fingers were too numb to feel the rescuing twigs, but I knew they were there and I knew they were stronger than they looked. Now I was able to kick at the sack. The struggle exhausted me and it must have taken five full minutes before it fell free of my feet at last.

I kicked tiredly towards the river bank and with the last of my strength I pulled myself up by the roots of the willow.

I tried to stand, but my frozen legs refused to obey me. Somehow I crawled upwards, through the undergrowth, towards the path and the bridge. If I had to crawl all the way back to Marsden Hall I'd do it. There was the path under my elbows and knees. Maybe someone will find me on the path! I thought. Then I decided there'd be no one here until daylight. I'd have died of the cold some time around midnight. I had to keep moving though every muscle in my body was rebelling and refusing to obey my mind.

I lay still for a few moments to gather my strength, but only grew colder and stiffer.

It was so unfair, I thought. I had escaped the river and now I was going to die alone and lonely on this path just half a mile from safety and warmth.

An owl hooted somewhere in the wood. Then a twig snapped. I thought I couldn't get any colder. But when that twig snapped I knew he'd come back to finish me off. I wished I'd let myself be drowned in the river. All that effort only to have my throat slit while I lay helpless at his feet.

Another soft footfall brought the feet level with my head. Bare feet. Small feet. A girl's feet. "William," Meg said. "Tell me you're not dead."

And I did something I'd never done since I was a child in skirts.

I cried.

CHAPTER SEVENTEEN

"I did but dream"

"I followed you as soon as I could," she explained as she walked me slowly along the path. I remembered how strong she was, and with my arm around her shoulder she was practically carrying me. But at last some warmth was returning to my legs as I walked and I was able to help myself after a few minutes.

"I didn't know where you'd gone, but I knew he'd taken you," she went on. "For some reason I headed for Bournmoor Woods and I saw him coming back. I was hiding behind a tree and he never saw me, but I guessed where he'd been. I thought I was too late … when I saw you there on the path … and then I heard you sob."

"I wasn't sobbing," I told her. "Just catching my breath."

"Of course!" she said.

"I was going to run after him and arrest him," I told her.

"That's what I thought you would do. Should I let you go now?"

"No!" I squawked rather too suddenly. I heard her chuckle. "Where are we headed?" I asked.

"To Widow Atkinson's cottage," she said. "You can't go home, not yet. He's still around. He wants to finish his plan and he won't let some boy stand in his way."

I limped alongside the girl as she guided me up the path

to the cottage. Mrs Atkinson still had a candle burning, and the warmth from her peat fire was the most welcoming I'd ever known. The old woman was more worried than I'd ever seen her. "It's all my fault," she mumbled, as she stripped wet clothes off me and wrapped me in a coarse woollen blanket that she used as a bedcover. "I knew he was a killer, but I didn't think anyone would believe me. I couldn't prove it."

"Don't worry, Mrs Atkinson," Meg said. "I worked it out too, but I didn't know what to do."

I looked into the glowing peat where Mrs Atkinson was stirring a brew of vegetables and herbs. "And I worked it out last of all!" I said. "But I think I can prove it."

"It was when your Great-Uncle George told the story of that Perkin Warbeck, wasn't it?" Meg said.

I nodded. "Perkin Warbeck *said* he was the Duke of York. People believed him because he said it. But it was a lie. And when the stranger arrived at Marsden Hall last night everyone *believed* he was Humphrey Vere, because he *told* us he was. It never occurred to us that he was a liar!"

"And a murderer," Meg said.

"And a murderer," I agreed.

Mrs Atkinson took a wooden bowl and filled it with soup from the pot. She handed it to me with a spoon. I tried to take it, but my hands were shaking too much. Meg took the bowl and spoon from her and began to feed me. There was no meat in the soup. I guessed that someone as poor as Widow Atkinson would hardly ever taste meat, but it began to warm me inside as soon as I swallowed the first spoonful.

"How do we explain it to your father?" Meg asked.

"Let's put the story together and see," I said.
"Humphrey Vere was a servant of the Queen working at
the Tower of London ... that part of the story is probably
true. He was a large man with straight fair hair and a
loyal man. He was a good choice to take secret messages
to King James in Scotland. He set out last week with his
passport – a passport that said Humphrey Vere was a tall
man with straight fair hair – and with packets of letters.
He was riding a grey horse."

"But Arbella Stuart's supporters knew about his journey," Meg said. "How could that happen?"

I shrugged. "They must have some spy at Elizabeth's
court, I guess. But that's something Secretary Cecil in
London needs to discover."

"So, the real Humphrey Vere set off from London with
his passport and his letters," Widow Atkinson said, taking up the story. "They couldn't just kill him because
Elizabeth would simply send more letters with enough
guards to make sure they got through to Scotland. They
had to send someone to kill Humphrey Vere ... and *then*
take his place!"

"That's right," I said. "A quiet spot in the north of England would be best. In the south there was a chance that someone might know the real Humphrey Vere."

"So the killer – your stranger guest – followed the real Humphrey Vere. He probably followed him from Durham. The stranger arrived last night with clean boots. He was supposed to have ridden all the way from York that day," Meg pointed out.

"The stranger saw his chance in Bournmoor Woods," I said between mouthfuls of soup. "He came up close behind Humphrey and probably chatted to him in a friendly way. Then, when the path was empty of any other travellers, he grabbed Vere, dragged him off his grey horse and strangled him. The stranger dragged the body through the herb patch and into the cover of some branches. He took the saddle-bag off the grey horse and sent the animal away with a slap. We know that Wat Grey found the horse and tried to disguise it, but that has nothing to do with the murder."

"I agree," Mrs Atkinson said. She filled the bowl with more soup, and this time I was able to drink it myself. "He searched through the letters and found the passport. If the body was found soon he could say, 'Ah! My letters! I'll take them to King James!' If the body *wasn't* found he could go back and collect them. But he *couldn't* risk the passport being found. That gave the wrong description. That passport had to disappear and he had to find some simple local magistrate to give him a new one."

"So, the stranger got rid of the passport and headed for the nearest manor house, Marsden Hall," Meg went on. "The killer said, 'I'm Humphrey Vere and I've been robbed of the Queen's letters.'"

"And we *believed* he was Humphrey Vere because he *said* he was," I groaned.

"But you were too clever for him," Mrs Atkinson said. I wasn't sure if she was talking about Meg or me. "You spotted that the saddle-bag had been carried on a grey horse – the *real* Humphrey Vere's horse. The dead Humphrey had grey hairs on his clothes, and there were grey hairs on the inner side of the saddle-bag, where it rests against the horse. The saddle-bag belonged to the dead man. He hadn't just stolen it from a man on a bay horse. And the killer didn't have time to switch the spare clothes from the other side of the pack. Those clothes also belonged to the real Humphrey Vere. They are far too big for the stranger who claims to be Humphrey."

"I thought the initial that was embroidered on the man's linen would prove it," Meg sighed. "I was confused when you said it didn't."

"I said what?"

"You said the letter was something called an 'aitch'," she reminded me.

"It is!" I said excitedly. "Aitch for Humphrey!"

Meg glared at me. "It's 'huh' for Humphrey."

"No!" I cried. "The letter is called 'aitch'."

"But you *say* it 'huh'?"

"Yes!"

"Why?"

"Why what?"

"Why do you *call* it 'aitch' but *say* it 'huh'?"

"I don't know!" I said.

She scowled into the peat fire. "No wonder it's impossible to read. It's like a secret code!"

"But that's what we need," I told her. "The saddle-bag

is at Marsden Manor. We'll show father the linen with the letter aitch and explain the truth. It's like the Perkin Warbeck story – once you see that the boy *isn't* the Duke of York then it all becomes clear. Even Father can understand that."

"The trouble is the stranger will kill you as soon as he sees you," Mrs Atkinson said. "Killing the Queen's messenger and plotting to steal her letters is probably treason. He won't just be hanged. He'll be taken back to London to be hanged, drawn and quartered. If the life of one boy can save him then he'll take that life."

"So, what do we do?" I asked.

"I think *I* have to do it," Meg said.

And so we arranged the trap for the next morning. Meg was making herself the bait in the trap, and I wasn't too happy with the thought. But Mrs Atkinson seemed to think that with my Great-Uncle George in Marsden Manor, the girl would be safe. "A great fighter, Sir George," she said.

My clothes had dried in front of the fire, but smelled like freshly baked bread! I slipped them back on and hurried home. I crept up a back stairway to the bedrooms, opened my door as softly as I could, closed it behind me and turned. The figure sitting on my bed made me jump. "Mother!" I gasped.

"Are you all right, William?" she asked.

"Fine," I said.

She looked at my stained clothes and back at my face. She was waiting for the truth. It was after midnight by now, but she didn't leave until I'd told her the full story. "I suppose I have to agree with your plan," she said finally. "Meg has a better chance of getting away with it than you do. But I want you to lock your door tonight. Our stranger may think you are dead, but he may just come here looking for those letters."

It was something I hadn't thought of and I was grateful for her common sense. She kissed me and left the room. I locked the door behind her, walked over to the bed and fell back into a deep and dreamless sleep.

The next morning the wind had swung round to the north and was stronger than ever. It tore at the remaining leaves on the trees and brought squally rain off the sea. "Not a good day for travelling," Great-Uncle George was saying. I had crept on to the balcony above the dining hall and watched as the family and our murderous guest gathered for breakfast.

Meg hurried around and served everyone. My mother turned to her. "Meg! Bring our guest a posset of hot wine to warm him before he leaves."

"So what do you think really happened to those Princes in the Tower, Sir George?" our guest asked.

"Murdered," the old knight replied. "Murdered by Sir James Tyrell that night when he took the keys. There is a story that he was arrested twenty years after the murders on another charge. He was sentenced to death and decided to confess everything before he died. He admitted that his henchmen had smothered the two little princes as they slept. Then they dug out a grave at the foot of a staircase and buried them deep under the floor. They must be still there now."

Meg returned and I watched her place the steaming drink in front of the guest. When he had swallowed half of it, she walked to the other end of the table and stood behind my father. "I want to report a murder," she said.

My father froze. "Go away, girl," he said through his teeth.

"Humphrey Vere, the Queen's messenger, was murdered in Bournmoor Woods," she persisted.

My father's face turned a strange purple colour. I glanced at the stranger and saw that the "V" of his lip was sharper than ever. My grandparents leaned forward eager for a little excitement, while Great-Uncle George and my mother smiled quiet encouragement at the girl. "Master Vere is alive and perfectly well, unless I'm very much mistaken," Father said stiffly.

"You are."

"What?"

"Very much mistaken," she said.

The stranger made a small movement of his hand towards his dagger. I knew from having fought him that he would be able to throw the dagger and strike her in the throat. He was sure he had killed me, and another corpse wouldn't matter too much to a man of cold blood.

From my hiding-place on the balcony the only sound I could hear was the furious snorting of air through my father's nostrils. He didn't look at her. "Get out and I will deal with you later," he said. The words all but choked him.

"Listen to her," my mother said quietly.

"You are responsible for the servants," he said to her. "You are to blame for this. Have her thrown out."

"Listen to her," Great-Uncle George said. My father hadn't the courage to bully the old knight.

"You tell him, George!" Grandmother cackled.

The stranger calmly sipped his wine. "Let's hear her story," he said.

And Meg repeated the story, smoothly and in every

detail as we'd rehearsed it in Widow Atkinson's cottage the long night before.

As she reached the end she produced a piece of theatre as dramatic as any Master Shakespeare planned on his London stages. From under her apron she pulled the linen undershirt with the initial "H" embroidered on it.

The stranger's cruel mouth turned down, his voice was soft and slurred. "That letter could stand for anything ... Henry or Harold. The man who robbed me had the same initial as me. So what?"

My father turned uncertainly to the serving girl. She told him, "The man must be guilty. Otherwise he wouldn't have tried to murder your son last night."

"Murder William? Where is the boy?" my father asked in a trembling voice.

"Safe," my mother said quickly and reached across the table to grasp his wrist.

The news seemed to make the decision for my father. He sat up stiffly and blinked. "I think Master Vere ... I mean Master whoever-you-are – that there is a case to answer."

"No proof," the man said dreamily.

"Enough to stop you going on to Edinburgh. Enough to hold you in Durham Castle until someone is sent from London to identify you or the corpse as Humphrey Vere," Great-Uncle George put in.

"If you had used my passport to get into James's palace, and then assassinated him, the Marsden family would have been ruined forever," my father said with a pained expression.

"And if King James VI of Scotland gets the throne then you'll be ruined anyway!" the man said, and he pushed at the arms of his chair as he struggled to rise.

My father shoved his chair back and jumped to his feet, frightened of the murderer. The man stood up and leaned against the table. He moved a hand towards his dagger, but he needed the hand to keep him on his feet. He swayed and clutched at the table edge again.

Meg walked slowly down the length of the table towards him. "Careful, girl!" my father gasped. But she placed her hands between the man's and knocked them sharply apart. Without the support of his arms he fell forward, his face smashing into the food bowl in front of him.

She walked on to the door and opened it. "Come in, Constable Smith," she said. "Sir James Marsden has a job for you."

The huge blacksmith shambled into the room and looked around warily. His eye caught the figure of the stranger, slumped over the table.

"Take that man, secure him with ropes and gather a few honest men. We are taking him to Durham Castle."

"Yes, sir," the smith said. "Why, sir?"

"Because he killed the man in Bournmoor Woods the day before yesterday," my father said proudly. "We didn't need the help of the village constable to track down the killer. I trapped him in my own home and arrested him."

The constable looked puzzled. "Did you knock him out too?" he asked.

"Ah, no … he appears to have been taken ill," my father said.

Meg slipped the small glass bottle from her apron. "I slipped a little of this herb into his wine," she explained. "Just enough to send him to sleep for a few hours."

"That's right," my mother put in. "We just wanted him to admit he was the killer – and we all heard him – but we didn't want him making a run for it."

"No, we didn't!" my father said. "Pick him up, Smith."

Before the constable reached the man he had slid sideways and on to the floor. "He tried to murder Master William!" Meg said furiously, and drew back her bare foot to kick the stranger in the face.

"Thank you, Meg!" my mother said. "I think we want him in a fit state to answer the questions of the Queen's ministers. He may find it hard if he wakes to discover his teeth missing." My mother buried her face in her embroidery and hid a smile.

I rose stiffly and walked downstairs.

"Lazarus risen from the dead!" Grandmother chuckled as she saw me.

The constable picked up the lifeless form of the killer and threw him over his shoulder, while Father announced he was off to arrange a horse to take him to Durham.

"That reminds me of a story," my grandmother said

dreamily.

"Tonight at dinner," Grandfather snapped. "We have a lot to do now. We need to collect the evidence, write statements and send messages to the Queen and her ministers in London."

"I was going to say that," my father muttered as he hurried through the door.

"In years to come this will make a good story," my mother said. She smiled at Grandmother. "And a happier one than the story of those two poor little Princes."

"But the story this reminds me of ..." Grandmother began.

"Tonight's the time for stories," Great-Uncle George said firmly, and for once his stepsister didn't argue.

I looked at Meg. Her green eyes glanced back from under the bramble-bush tangle of hair. "But this story seems to have ended rather well," she said.

The autumn wind rattled the doors on the old hall and I knew that one day I would have to tell the story again. Meg's story – my story – the story of the Princes in the Tower.

People die ... even princes and patchwork pretenders.

In time old houses crumble ... but stories live forever.

The Historical Characters

The Marsden family are fictional, but the main events in Anthony Marsden's story really took place and some of the characters in the story were real people.

EDWARD V The young king who was never crowned. When his father, Edward IV, died, Edward was proclaimed king, but he mysteriously disappeared when his Uncle Richard sent him to the Tower of London. Bad health and the life in the tower made him a gloomy boy.

RICHARD, DUKE OF YORK Edward's younger brother. Went to the Tower of London to prepare for Edward V's coronation, but vanished at the same time as his brother. While he was alive he seems to have been more cheerful in the Tower than his brother.

RICHARD III Brother of the dead king, Edward IV. But while Edward had been tall, fair and handsome, Richard was small, dark and possibly had a withered arm. This did not prevent him becoming a powerful fighter in battle. He took charge of the new young king, Edward V, and then told the English people that there had been a mistake: Edward was not really king. Richard had himself crowned instead.

DUKE OF BUCKINGHAM One of the most important noblemen in England. A proud man, jealous of the power of others. A great supporter of Richard III until Richard was crowned. For some reason, no one is sure why, they fell out and Buckingham turned traitor.

ROBERT BRACKENBURY Made Constable of the Tower of London where he guarded the Princes, helped by just four men, Will Slaughter, Miles Forrest and two others whose names we don't know. (In the story one of the men is Anthony Marsden.) Loyal to Richard to the end, when he died beside him at the battle of Bosworth Field.

JAMES TYRELL "Master of the King's Henchmen" and one of Richard III's oldest and most trusted servants. He was just the sort of man that Richard would ask to murder the Princes. Tyrell was arrested almost twenty years after the Princes disappeared and sentenced to death. It's said that before he was executed he confessed to murdering the Princes by smothering them in their mattress.

HENRY TUDOR Invaded England and defeated Richard III at Bosworth Field to become King Henry VII. He was tall, slim and fair with grey eyes and bad teeth. He was clever, ruthless and very careful with his money. He made England peaceful and rich.

PERKIN WARBECK A young man who worked for a Flemish cloth merchant. When he went to Ireland someone thought he looked like the dead prince and hatched the plot to overthrow Henry VII. A handsome young man with long fair hair and a good actor. In the end he proved to be a bit of a coward and was executed by Henry VII.

The Time Trail

1483 9 April King Edward IV dies in London, leaving the kingdom to his eldest son, Edward, Prince of Wales.

11 April The twelve-year-old-boy is proclaimed Edward V, but he is in Ludlow. He needs to travel to London to be crowned, so ...

24 April ... young Edward sets off with his uncle, Lord Rivers, for London. By ...

30 April ... the new king arrives in Stony Stratford. His Uncle Richard meets him here, locks up Lord Rivers and takes charge. He escorts the boy to the Tower of London and keeps him there for safety. The coronation is set for 22 June, but on ...

16 June ... Edward and his younger brother are moved into the Bloody Tower while their Uncle Richard cancels the coronation. Then on ...

26 June ... Uncle Richard has himself declared King Richard III and on ...

6 July ... Richard is crowned with his queen, Anne. While Richard and Anne tour the country ...

3 September ... the King's trusted servant Sir James Tyrell visits London and asks the Constable of the Tower to hand over the keys. The Princes in the Tower are never seen alive again after this. But Richard will have no peace.

24 September The Duke of Buckingham, Richard's former friend, invites Henry Tudor to invade England, fight Richard III and take his throne. Bad weather wrecks the invasion plans, but Richard has more bad luck when …

1484 9 April … his son dies, and …

1485 16 March … his queen, Anne, dies. The Henry Tudor invasion arrives and on …

1485 22 August … Henry defeats Richard at Bosworth Field and takes the crown. But …

1486 … in summer, plotting begins to replace Henry Tudor with young men who will pretend to be one of the Princes in the Tower. Henry defeats them all. In …

1487 16 June … the Pretender Lambert Simnel's army is massacred at Stoke, and …

1496 September … the Pretender Perkin Warbeck is defeated when he invades the north of England with the help of the Scots.

1499 23 November Perkin Warbeck is executed. Pretenders get the message and there are no more. The Tudors rule for another hundred years till Henry VII's granddaughter, Elizabeth I, dies in …

1603 … and James of Scotland takes the English throne.

But it's not quite the end of the story because …

1674 17 July … as the Tower of London is being altered the skeletons of two children are uncovered, the taller child on its back, the smaller face down on top of it. Scientists and historians are still arguing about whether these could be the bodies of the Princes who were murdered in the Tower. Perhaps we'll never know for certain.

Tudor Terror

The King in Blood Red and Gold

When handsome, foppish Hugh Richmond turns up at Marsden Manor, claiming to be one of Queen Elizabeth's spies asking for help, Will and his grandfather seize on the chance for adventure!

Riding north to Scotland, Grandfather tells Will how his own father fought at the Battle of Flodden Field in the service of Henry VIII. Then as now, there were desperate skirmishes on the Borders between the English and the Scots Reivers – cattle thieves.

Neither of them realise quite what danger Hugh is leading them into ... and it seems that all their quick wit and courage will not get them out.

Luckily, Meg the serving girl is very clever ...

Two interwoven stories of battle and adventure,
each as exciting as the other.

Coming soon

The Lady of Fire and Tears
The Knight of Stars and Storms
The Lord of the Dreaming Globe
The Queen of the Dying Light